# CIRCLES
# OF STONE

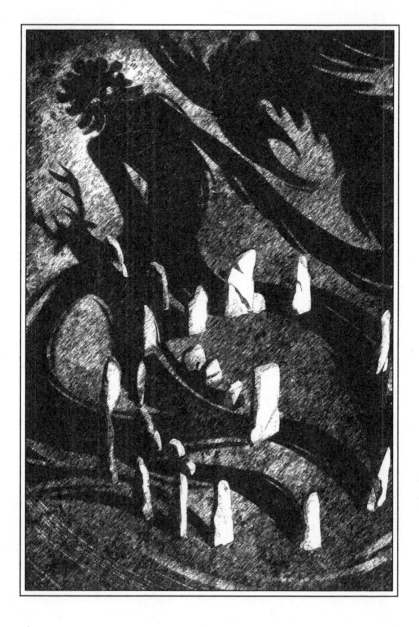

# CIRCLES OF STONE

## Weird Tales of Pagan Sites and Ancient Rites

*edited by*
KATY SOAR

This edition published 2023 by
The British Library
96 Euston Road
London NW1 2DB

Cataloguing in Publication Data
A catalogue record for this publication is available from the British Library

ISBN 978 0 7123 5459 2
e-ISBN 978 0 7123 6861 2

Frontispiece illustration by Sandra Gómez. The photographs on pages 6
and 240 (Jonny Davidson, 2023) show views of Harold's Stones at Trellech,
Monmouthshire (Gwent), a village which is thought to take its name from
the stones ('Tre (Tri)': 'three' or 'town' + 'llech': 'flat stone' or 'slate').

Cover design by Mauricio Villamayor with illustration by Sandra Gómez
Text design and typesetting by Tetragon, London
Printed in England by CPI Group (UK) Ltd, Croydon, CRO 4YY

# CONTENTS

# INTRODUCTION

The first lines of "The Ruin", an Old English poem of the tenth century CE, describe old stones as "Wrætlic". Usually translated as "wondrous", Peter Ackroyd has read the line as "wraith-like": "wraith-like is this native stone". While the poem itself discusses the masonry of a crumbling Roman town, the phrase itself is certainly apt for thinking about the megalithic monuments that cover the British Isles. These native stones—stone circles, stone rows, standing stones (or menhirs), and dolmens—are indeed wraith-like, spectral, haunted. Standing for thousands of years within the landscape, their physical presence is evocative but their original purpose is tantalisingly vague. With no written records to inform us as to how and why they were initially built, they become a nexus for stories. And as the examples in this collection show, those stories are—more frequently than not—wraith-like.

The stories in this collection reflect many of the popular beliefs and narratives that developed around these stones over the centuries, both about their origin and their purpose. The first piece, an excerpt from the novella *Ringstones* by Sarban, sets up some of these ideas, neatly encapsulating the divide between "academic" and "popular" opinion—were stone circles temples for sun worship, or were they built by magical beings? The extract, however, ends with an ambiguous statement which highlights the ongoing mysterious nature of these sites.

Many various historical civilisations and groups were considered as their constructors: Phoenicians, Romans, Danes, Saxons, Egyptians, Chaldeans, even native Americans. But from the seventeenth century in particular, the favoured architects of these monuments were the Druids. Antiquarians such as Hector Boecce, John Aubrey and William

Stukeley made the druidical connection to stone monuments, particularly Stonehenge, explicit. Druids were perfect for stone circles—like the stones themselves, they were ambiguous and mysterious, and were considered both as mystical philosopher priests who built stone circles as solar or astronomical temples and as barbarous savages who practised human sacrifices at the sites in honour of their bloodthirsty gods, rendering these sites places of both wonder and horror. While the connection between Druids and stone monuments dissipated within academic circles with advances in archaeological knowledge from the mid nineteenth century, the idea never really faded from the popular imagination.

Developing alongside the more academic debate regarding the originators of these stone monuments were folkloric and popular traditions regarding their development and purpose. These motifs and themes often reflect (contemporary) fears, tensions or beliefs, to which these stones act as a kind of nexus. Magical, folkloric creatures were often associated with these sites; giants, fairies, witches, and the devil have all been connected to megaliths and stone circles.

Given the colossal nature of many of the monuments, it is unsurprising that giants were often considered to be behind their construction. In 1136, Geoffrey of Monmouth in his *Historia Regum Britanniae* described how Merlin created Stonehenge by moving the Giants' Ring from Mount Killaraus in Ireland to Salisbury Plain—showing that the fantastical and magical have long been associated with these stones and their construction. He also attributed its original construction in Ireland to giants who brought the stones from Africa to Mount Killaraus. This colossal origin is reflected in the name Geoffrey gave to the structure—the Giant's Dance.

Fairies have been associated with barrows since the twelfth century, but some megaliths also have fae connections: stone circles and standing stones were thought to mark the entrance to their realm. For example, the King Stone from the Rollright Stones in Oxfordshire is said to mark the entrance to the fairy kingdom beneath the circle. The devil has made a more recent appearance. By the mid eighteenth century, Stukeley reports that the stones in the northern inner circle of Avebury (the Cove) were known as the Devil's Brand-Irons, and that Stonehenge's Heel Stone was created when "the devil threw it at the builders". Many of these traditions which associated megalithic monuments with the devil were originally associated with giants, and only latterly with Old Nick himself, showing how associations change depending on historical and social contexts. And where the devil goes, so too do witches. Stone circles were thought to be sites where witches would meet to practise their infernal rites. Isobel Gowdie, a seventeenth-century Scottish woman accused of witchcraft, noted in her confession that her and other witches would shoot elf-arrows at "the standing-stanes" at Auldern, where the devil would "sit on a blak kist", presumably the remains of the prehistoric ring-cairn that was once in the centre of the four stones.

These often-infernal associations could also be used as cautionary tales. The motif of petrification usually viewed stones as the remains of trespassers turned to stone for their digressions, particularly against God and the sabbath. For example, the stones of the Callanish circle in the Outer Hebrides were the petrified bodies of giants who had refused to accept Christianity, while the Nine Ladies in Derbyshire are nine women and a fiddle player who were turned to stone for dancing on a Sunday. This was a particularly prominent folk idea during the seventeenth century, and may in part have been inspired by a campaign against Sunday games and dances which began under Elizabeth I. But this punishment wasn't just related to Christianity: a petrified witch stands at the centre of Mitchell's Fold Stone circle, turned into such for milking a magical cow dry, the surrounding stones set up to fence her in.

The stones were also thought to have a degree of agency. To tamper with or damage these stones was to court ill luck. In 1861 J. T. Blight, a Cornish archaeological artist, reported that the man responsible for pulling down a cromlech near Manyon in Cornwall began to suffer from misfortunes, such as his cattle dying and his crops failing. Many stones are also thought to be able to move by themselves, to turn round, turn over, or dance. Visiting water also seems to be a common theme: Maen Ceti, a Neolithic chambered cairn in West Glamorgan, is said to rise and go to the sea to bathe at Midsummer Eve and All-Hallow's Eve.

The stories in this volume range from the 1890s to 2018 and encompass many of these druidical ideas in a variety of forms, often adding a contemporary or individual twist to the traditional motifs. The idea that stone circles and megaliths were built by pagan, often Druid, priests and used for sacrificial rites appears in a number of these stories; sometimes these practices are inadvertently resurrected in the contemporary world, as in the stories by E. F. Benson and Jasper John, or, as those by H. R. Wakefield and Algernon Blackwood show, the protagonist realises too late that the practices never actually ended, or are destined to be played out forever. These ideas about their construction also combine with the folkloric traditions regarding giants, witches and the devil, as in the tales from Stuart Strauss and Frederick Cowles. Academic theory also sought to explain away some of the more magical beliefs regarding ancient sites; later nineteenth-century ideas about fairies often considered them to be an earlier race of "primitive human" who had survived into the present, living in hidden places at the edges of civilisation—a theme common in the work of Arthur Machen, and inferred in his story included in this collection. Mary Williams' tale too deals with these primeval, elemental forces. Local as well as more general beliefs are often intertwined; for example, in the West Country, it was believed that witches were not predominantly female, but could just as likely be a man, a motif that plays out in J. H. Pearce's Cornish-set tale. Cornwall, unsurprisingly given the vast amount of megaliths that dot the landscape, appears as a setting in several other tales, such as Williams' mentioned above, and the story by A. L. Rowse. Here, we see the agency—perhaps even conscious-ness—of the stones, when a standing stone begins to haunt and to threaten a young boy who takes an interest in it.

Both Nigel Kneale and L. T. C. Rolt also address the agency of the stones, particularly in regard to their ability to bring misfortune to those who try and displace them, but give them a distinctly twentieth-century twist. Similarly, both Lisa Tuttle and Elsa Wallace's tales tell us why it behoves us to leave standing stones well alone, and provide novel approaches to the motifs of movement and petrification; Tuttle's tale in particular reminds us that distance may be no challenge to these stones...

As the stories in this volume show, who built the stones and what they were meant for continue to fascinate us despite advances in archaeological practice and theory. These monuments appear in some ways inexplicable, and when faced with this, we are compelled to create stories to explain them. What this collection shows is that these enigmatic monuments continue to captivate and enthral, and that magic and the supernatural cling to these places still.

KATY SOAR

## FURTHER READING AND REFERENCES

Ackroyd, Peter, *The English Ghost: Spectres Through Time* (London: Vintage Books, 2010).

Burl, Aubrey, *John Aubrey and Stone Circles: Britain's First Archaeologist* (Gloucester: Amberley Publishing, 2010).

Grinsell, Leslie V., *Folklore of Prehistoric Sites in Britain* (London: David and Charles, 1976).

Harte, Jeremy, *Cloven Country: The Devil and the English Landscape* (London: Reaktion Books, 2022).

Hutton, Ronald, "Megaliths and Memory", in Parker, Joanne (ed.), *Written on Stone: The Cultural Reception of British Prehistoric Monuments* (Newcastle: Cambridge Scholars Publishing, 2009), 10–22.

Michell, John, *Megalithomania* (London: Thames and Hudson, 1982).

# A NOTE FROM THE PUBLISHER

The original short stories reprinted in the British Library Tales of the Weird series were written and published in a period ranging across the nineteenth and twentieth centuries. There are many elements of these stories which continue to entertain modern readers; however, in some cases there are also uses of language, instances of stereotyping and some attitudes expressed by narrators or characters which may not be endorsed by the publishing standards of today. We acknowledge therefore that some elements in the stories selected for reprinting may continue to make uncomfortable reading for some of our audience. With this series British Library Publishing aims to offer a new readership a chance to read some of the rare material of the British Library's collections in an affordable paperback format, to enjoy their merits and to look back into the worlds of the past two centuries as portrayed by their writers. It is not possible to separate these stories from the history of their writing and as such the following stories are presented as they were originally published with one edit to the text and with minor edits made for consistency of style and sense. We welcome feedback from our readers, which can be sent to the following address:

British Library Publishing
The British Library
96 Euston Road
London, NW1 2DB
United Kingdom

## AN EXTRACT FROM
# RINGSTONES

## *Sarban*

Sarban was the pen name for the British diplomat John W. Wall (1910–1989). For over 30 years, between 1933 and 1966, Wall was stationed at various diplomatic outposts in the Middle East, as well as Paraguay. During the 1950s, he released three books—*Ringstones, and Other Curious Tales* (1951), *The Sound of His Horn* (1952), and *The Doll Maker, and Other Tales of the Uncanny* (1953), all published by Peter Davis. His novellas and short stories often share similar themes, many of which deal with the survival of the mythical past and the threat this poses in the present, and frequently have a sexual undercurrent. Through a framing device, *Ringstones* tells the story of Daphne Hazel, a student teacher hired by the reclusive and eccentric Dr Ravelin to tutor the three young mysterious and foreign children staying with him at Ringstones Hall on the Northumbrian Moors for the summer, and whom, according to the doctor, "belong to some very old friends of mine". Ravelin is fascinated by the ancient past of the landscape surrounding the house, which takes its name from the nearby stone circle, where, on a trip out from the Hall, the doctor recounts to Daphne the various ideas behind the purpose and role of stone circles.

**W**hen we reached the moor Dr Ravelin's keenness redoubled with the difficulty of his task. For there, try as hard as I might, I could not make out, across the billows of heather and the natural dips and rises of the moor, the traces of the broad way which he declared had led in ancient times direct from the top of the causeway to the Stone Circle. True, here and there a grey old stone did hump its back above the green, brown and purple sea, but it needed far more faith or training than I possessed to build out of those such a stately avenue of monoliths as Dr Ravelin wanted me to see. And then, I don't think I wanted to picture it like that; I liked the moor better for its wildness. Yet when we reached the low flat hillock on which the Stone Circle stands, I think that even without Dr Ravelin's guidance I should have been impressed by the recognition of human traces in a place where human beings seemed so out of place. As we came up out of the waist-deep heather on to that crown of smooth sward from which nothing of the Park is visible we stood still. The two girls and Katia slipped off their shoes, invited I suppose by the pleasant turf, but for an instant it seemed like a gesture of reverence; I almost looked to see Dr Ravelin put off the shoes from his feet.

Instead, using his stick as a teacher's pointer, he began very briskly to lecture on the plan of the area. I listened with only half my attention. For one thing, I was watching Marvan and Ianthe. Far from showing any reverence they seemed to have gone mad as soon as we got inside the Stone Circle, and while I followed Dr Ravelin sedately on his tour of the ancient monument they were capering about, dancing on the fallen stones, calling and shrieking to each other and generally behaving like chimpanzees in church. For the rest, I don't think I had any real interest in Dr Ravelin's information about dimensions, dates, orientations and comparisons with this and the other stone circle in places I had never heard of. I was content to saunter along with him over that deep, soft turf and drink in the still, brooding beauty of the place, its drowsy warmth of sunlit but soft greens and browns, the ancient stones, their hardness mantled with moss and a gold lace of lichen, dreaming there as though to idle through eternity in the sunlight; the rich blue sky above us, the scent of wild thyme and sun-warmed peat, and the faint summer song of insects.

But Katia was a practical girl. She began spreading out the tea, and chose for a table the very stone, a smaller, horizontal one at the bottom of the horseshoe formed by the standing monoliths, about which Dr Ravelin was just then discoursing.

"Not here, please," he said, smiling and removing the basket to the ground. "Archaeologists have been accused by sentimental persons of having no reverence for the bones of the heathen. Let us at least redeem our reputation by sparing the Altar Stone the desecration of our bakelite and buns."

Katia's eyes were just blue blanks of incomprehension, but after an appealing look at me in vain, she hitched up her dress and squatted cross-legged on the turf, inviting us with a sweep of her hand to range ourselves within reach of the eatables.

Dr Ravelin talked as we ate. "You see," he remarked when we had settled ourselves with our backs to the Altar Stone, "that the next horizontal stone before us—that one beyond the gap in the circle—the Sun Stone as it is called—is exactly in line with the lowest point in the Eastern ridge there. On June twenty-first the sun is first seen exactly in the centre of that dip in the hill. We have no true horizon here, so the altar is oriented on the apparent point of sunrise on Midsummer day. That is the argument for the heliacal character of the rites for which the circle was set up. So, it is supposed, some comparative limits in time for the construction of the circle can be inferred. The sun does not begin to reign over mythology until a fairly late stage in human history: until kings and warrior castes are firmly established in the direction of affairs. If that argument is sound surely the children of the sun never carried their golden legend into a stranger place than this. Except in such a rare summer as this, all about here is a cloudy wilderness of shadows: you would say the edge of the dark underworld of Hades rather than a bright arena of the sun."

I lay leaning on my elbow, enjoying the blaze of the sun on my body and looking through half-closed lids at the golden-skinned girls to whom, in the bright simplicity of their white dresses, that phrase "children of the sun" seemed so appropriately to apply.

"Perhaps," I said, "they brought the sun with them, like Nuaman. He says the sun shines for him. Perhaps it really would shine for people who worshipped it. I feel I could worship it myself on such a day."

"Undoubtedly they brought him," said Dr Ravelin. "That is to say, they brought his worship. But why should the importers or inheritors of an elaborate solar cult pitch on such an unlikely place for their temple? Why should they go to the labour and expense of raising a stone circle here where it must be oriented on a sunrise which they knew was not the true sunrise? The answer must be a guess. Analogy helps. In Mecca that stone cube sacred to the heathen idols of Arabia became the holy house of Allah; in Cordova the moslem mosque became the Christian cathedral; in Lebanon I have seen in a niche in the foundations of a Greek temple a modern print of the Virgin; and I have seen a French-minted piastre-piece hung as a votive offering on a branch of a fig-tree by that fountain of Adonis which the people now call the River of Abraham. As new religion ousts the old it tenants the latter's temples. It is good strategy. A god turned out of doors commands little respect. But also, the conqueror sits on the vanquished's throne because it is a throne. The Lebanese peasant who climbs the rugged valley to make his offering to the Virgin at Artemis's shrine knows nothing about Artemis and not much about the Virgin; what he does know is that the *place* is holy. We cannot even guess much about who came here before these stones were raised but one thing we can guess: that it was a holy place before they planted these stones."

I listened lazily. "Somebody must have made it holy, I suppose," I said, "if *they* didn't." I wasn't at all clear who "they" were. "Hasn't anyone ever suggested that it was the fairies who made these places? This is exactly what I should imagine a fairies' dancing-floor to be like."

"Ah!" exclaimed the Doctor with a note of approval. "You favour the older school of thought, do you? Elves, fairies, giants, magicians—certainly not just ordinary human beings must have raised these circles. That was the old belief. In Welsh legend there is an account of the origin of Stonehenge which attributes it to Aurelius Ambrosius, who may or may not be a legendary figure himself. Though there is evidence to suggest that Stonehenge was built at least two thousand years before Aurelius Ambrosius, yet the legend is interesting because it hints, in a poetical way, at something towards which archaeological discovery seems also to point. According to the legend, Aurelius Ambrosius ordered the magician Merlin to build him a stone circle on Salisbury Plain. Merlin, with a regard for economy which is entirely convincing, produced one out of stock. That is, by the power of incantation he removed one which already existed in Ireland and planted it down on Salisbury Plain. Now the interesting thing is that the legend also says that that same circle had been brought to Ireland by giants who carried it there out of Africa. Well, what is that but a way of saying that sun-worship and sun-temples were dimly remembered as an importation?"

"Still," I felt able to point out, "even though Merlin or some other magician had dumped this one down here, it doesn't explain why he chose this particular spot, which, you say, isn't the right sort of place."

"No," said Dr Ravelin, "it doesn't. And there my theory seems to offer the only possible explanation. A church chooses to sit upon a heathen temple. Perhaps these ancient stones hold down something far more ancient, something far stranger than the men who placed them understood. Some queer feet have danced here, I feel."

# THE TEMPLE

## E. F. Benson

Edward Frederic Benson (1867–1940) will be a name familiar to many fans of weird tales, although he is primarily known for his Mapp and Lucia series of novels. While a student of Classics at Cambridge, he was good friends with M. R. James, and from 1892 to 1895 he was a member of the British School at Athens, and he later worked for the Hellenic Society in Egypt. His archaeological knowledge and background appears in several of his short stories. Cornwall is also frequently the setting of his works, drawing on his own upbringing (his father was bishop of Truro from 1877–1883). The stone monuments of Cornwall had long been considered sites of druidical ritual; for example, in his 1754 work *The Antiquities of Cornwall,* the Rev. William Borlase linked prehistoric sites in Cornwall with scenes of human sacrifice, and this was something Benson drew on for his novel *Raven's Brood* (1934), and again for the story reproduced here, which was published in *Hutchinson's Magazine* in November 1924.

F rank Ingleton and I had left London early in July with the intention of spending a couple of months at least in Cornwall. This sojourn was not by any means to be a complete holiday, for he was a student of those remains of prehistoric civilisation which are found in such mysterious abundance in the ancient county, and I was employed on a book which should have already been approaching completion, but which was still lamentably far from its consummation. Naturally there was to be a little golf and a little sea-bathing for relaxation, but we were both keen on our work and meant to have gathered in a respectable harvest of industry before we returned.

The village of St Caradoc, from all accounts, seemed likely to be favourable to our projects, for there were remains in the neighbourhood which had never been thoroughly investigated by any archæologist, and its position on the map, remote from any of the more celebrated holiday centres, promised a reasonable tranquillity. It supplied also the desirable relaxations; the club-house of a pleasantly hazardous golf-court stood at the bottom of the hotel garden, and five minutes' walk across the sand-dunes among which the holes were placed, led to the beach. The hotel was comfortable, and at present half-empty, and fortune seemed to smile on our undertakings. We settled down, therefore, without further plans. Frank meant, before he left, to visit other parts of the county, but here, within a mile of the hotel, was that curious circle of monoliths, like some Stonehenge in miniature, known as the "Council of Penruth." It had always been supposed, so Frank told me, that it was some place of Druidical worship, but he distrusted the conclusion and wanted to study it minutely on the spot.

I went there with him by way of an evening saunter on the second day after our arrival. The shortest way was along the sand-dunes, and thence up a steep, grassy slope on to the ploughed stretches of the uplands. In that warm, soft climate the wheat was in full ear, and beginning already to turn ripe and tawny. A very narrow path led across these cornfields to our destination, and from far off one could see the circle of stones, four to five feet high, standing there, black and austere, against the yellowing grain. Though all the country round was in cultivation, no plough had furrowed the interior of the circle, and inside was the ancient turf of the downs, short and velvety, with patches of thyme and hare-bells. It seemed odd; a plough could have passed backwards and forwards between the monoliths, and a half acre of land have been made fruitful.

"But why isn't it ploughed?" I asked.

"Oh, you're in the land of superstitions and ancient sorceries," he said. "These circles are never touched or made use of. And do you see, the path across the fields by which we have come, passes round it; it doesn't run across it. There it goes again on the far side, pursuing the same line, after making the detour."

He laughed.

"The farmer of the land was up here this morning when I was making some measurements," he said. "He went round it, I noticed, and when his dog came inside after some interesting smell, he called it back, and cuffed it, and rapped out: 'Come out of that there; and never do you go within again.'"

"But what's the idea?" I asked.

"Something clings to it, some curse, some abomination. They think no doubt, just as the archæologists do, that the place has been a

Druidical temple, where dreadful rites were performed, and human sacrifices made. But they are all wrong; this was never a temple at all, it was a Council Chamber, and the very name of it, the 'Council of Penruth,' confirms that. No doubt there was a temple somewhere about; dearly should I like to find it."

It had been hot work climbing up that steep, slippery hillside from the village, and we sat down within the circle, leaning our backs against two adjacent stones, and as we sat and rested, Frank explained to me the grounds of his belief.

"If you care to count them," he said, "you'll find there are twenty-one of these monoliths, against two of which you and I are leaning, and if you care to measure the distances between them, you will find that they are all equal. Each stone, in fact, represents the seat of a member of the council of twenty-one. But if the place had been a temple there would have been a larger gap between two of the stones towards the east, where the gate of the temple was, facing the rising sun, and somewhere within the circle, probably exactly in the middle, there would have been a large, flat stone, which was the stone of sacrifice, where no doubt human victims were offered. Or, if the stone had disappeared, there would have been a depression where it once was. Those are the distinguishing marks of a temple, and this place lacks them. It has always been assumed that it was a temple, and it has been described as such. But I am sure I am right about it."

"But there is a temple somewhere about?" I asked.

"Certain to be. If any of these prehistoric settlements was large enough to have a council hall, it would certainly have had a temple, though the remains of it have very likely disappeared. When the country was Christianised, the old religion—if you can call it a religion—was reckoned an abomination, and the places of worship were destroyed, just as the Israelites destroyed the groves of Baal. But I mean to explore very thoroughly here: there may be remains in some of those woods down there. This is just the sort of remote place where the temple might have escaped destruction."

"And what was the ancient religion?" I asked.

"Very little is known about it. It certainly was a religion not of love but fear. The gods were the blind powers of nature, manifesting themselves in storms and destruction and plague, and had to be propitiated with human sacrifices. And the priests, of course, dealt in magic and sorcery. They were the governing class, and kept their power alive by terror. If you offended them, as likely as not you would be sent for, and told that the gods required your eldest son as a blood-offering next midsummer day at sunrise when the first beams of morning shone through the eastern gate of the temple. It was wise to be a good churchman in those days."

"It looks a kindly country nowadays," I said. "The temples of the old gods are empty."

"Yes, but it's extraordinary how old superstitions linger. It isn't a year ago that there was a witchcraft trial in Penzance. The cattle belonging to some farmer near here began to pine and die, and he went to an old woman who said that a spell had been cast on them, and that if he paid her she could remove it. He went on paying and paying and at last got tired of that and prosecuted her instead."

He looked at his watch.

"Let's take a stroll before dinner," he said. "Instead of going back the way we came, we might make a ramble down the hillside in front and through the woods. They look rather attractive."

"And may conceal a pagan temple," said I, getting up.

We skirted the harvest fields, and found a path leading through a big fir-wood that climbed up the hillside. The trees were of no great growth as regards height, and the prevalent wind from the south-west, to which they stood exposed, had combed and pressed their branches landwards. But the foliage of the tree-tops was very dense, making a curious sombre twilight as we penetrated deeper into the wood. There was no undergrowth whatever below them, the ground was spread thick and smooth in fallen pine needles, and with the tree trunks rising straight and column-like and that thick roof of branches above, the place looked like some great hall of nature's building. No whisper of wind moved overhead, and so dark and still was it, that you might easily have conceived yourself to be walking up the aisle of some walled-in place. The smell of the firs was thick in the air like incense, and the foot went noiselessly as over spread carpets. No birds flitted between the tree trunks or called to each other, the only noise was the murmurous buzz of flies, which sounded like some long-held organ note.

It had been hot enough outside in the fresh draught off the sea, but here where no breeze winnowed the air it was stiflingly close, and as we plunged deeper into the dimness I was conscious of some gathering oppression of the spirit. It was an uncomfortable place, it seemed thick with unseen presences. And the same notion must have struck Frank as well.

"I feel as if we were being watched," he said. "There are eyes peeping at us from behind the trunks, and they don't like us. Now what makes so silly an idea to enter my head?"

"A grove of Baal is it?" I suggested. "One that has escaped destruction and is full of the spirits of murderous priests."

"I wish it was," he said. "Then we could inquire the way to the temple."

Suddenly he pointed ahead.

"Hullo, what's that?" he said.

I followed the direction of his finger, and for one half-second thought I saw the glimmer of something white moving among the trees.

But before I could focus it, it was gone. Somehow, the heat and the oppression had got on my nerves.

"Well, it's not our wood," I said. "I suppose other people have just as much right to walk here. But I've had enough of tree-trunks, I should like to have done with the wood."

Even as I spoke, I saw it was getting lighter in front of us; glimmers of day began to show between the thickset trunks, and presently we found ourselves threading the last row of the trees. The light of day poured in again and the stir of the sea breeze; it was like coming out of some crowded and airless building into the open air.

We emerged into a delectable place; a broad stretch of downland turf was spread in front of us, smooth and ancient turf like that in the Circle, jewelled with thyme and centaury and bugloss. The path we had been following lay straight across this, and dipping down over the edge of it we came suddenly on the most enchanting little house, low and two-storied, standing in a small enclosure of lawn and garden beds. The hill behind it had evidently once been quarried, but long ago, for now the sheer sides of it were overgrown with a tangle of ivy and briony, and at their base lay a pool of water. Beyond and bordering the lawn was a copse of birches and hornbeams, which half encircled the clearing in which stood house and garden. The house itself, half smothered in honeysuckle and climbing fuchsia seemed unoccupied, for the chimneys were smokeless and the blinds drawn down over the windows. As we turned the corner of its low fence and came on to the front of it, the impression was verified, for there by the gate was a notice proclaiming that it was to be let furnished, and directing that application should be made to a house agent in St Caradoc's.

"But it's a pocket Paradise," said I. "Why shouldn't we—"

Frank interrupted me.

"Of course there's no reason why we shouldn't," he said. "In fact, there's every reason why we should. The manager at the hotel told me they were filling up next week and wanted to know for how long we should stop. We'll make inquiries tomorrow morning, and find the agent and the keys."

The keys next morning revealed a charm within that came up to the promise of what we had seen without, and, what was as wonderful, the agent could provide our staff as well. This consisted of a rotund and capable Cornish-woman who, with her daughter to help her, would arrive early every morning, and remain till she had served our dinner, and then go back to her cottage in St Caradoc's. If that would suffice us, she was ready to be in charge as soon as we settled to take the little house; it must be understood, however, that she would not sleep there. Without making any further inquiries, the assurance that she was a clean and capable cook and competent in every way was enough, and two days afterwards we entered into possession. The rent asked was extraordinarily low, and my suspicious mind, as we went through the house, visualised an absence of water-supply or a kitchen range that, while getting red hot, left its ovens as in the chill of an Arctic night. But no such dispiriting discoveries awaited us; Mrs Fennell turned taps and manipulated dampers, and, scouring capably through the house, pronounced on her solemn guarantee that we should be very comfortable. "But I go back to my own house at night, gentlemen," she said, "and I promise you the water will be hot and your breakfast ready for you by eight in the morning."

We entered that afternoon; our luggage had been sent up an hour before, and when we arrived the portmanteaux were already unpacked, and clothes bestowed in their drawers, and tea ready in the sitting-room. It and its adjoining dining-room with a small parqueted hall, formed the ground floor accommodation. Beyond the dining-room was the kitchen, the convenience of which had already satisfied Mrs Fennell. Upstairs there were two good bedrooms, and above the kitchen two smaller servants' rooms, which, by our arrangement, would be unoccupied. There was a bathroom between the two bedrooms with a door into it from each; for two friends occupying the house nothing could have been more exactly what was wanted with nothing to spare. Mrs Fennell gave us an admirable plain dinner, and by nine o'clock she had locked the outer kitchen door and left us.

Before going to bed we wandered out into the garden, marvelling at our luck. The hotel, as the manager had told us, was already beginning to fill up, the dining-room tonight would have been a cackle of voices, the sitting-room crowded, and surely it was a wonderfully good exchange to be housed in this commodious little tranquillity of a place, with our own unobtrusive establishment that came at dawn and left at night. It remained only to see if this paragon who was so proficient in her kitchen would be as punctual in the morning.

"But I wonder why she and her daughter would not establish themselves here," said Frank. "They live alone down in the village. You'd have thought that they would have shut their cottage up, and saved themselves a morning and evening tramp."

"Gregariousness," said I. "They like to know that there are people, just people, close at hand and to right and left. I like to know that there are not. I like—"

As I spoke we turned at the garden gate, where the notice that the house was to let had been, and my eyes, quite idly, travelled across the space of open downland to the black fringe of the wood that stood above it, and for a moment, bright, and then quenched again like the line of fire made by a match that has been struck and has not flared, I saw a light there. It was only for a second that it was visible, but it must have been somewhere inside the wood, for against that luminous streak I saw the shape of the fir trunks.

"Did you see that?" I said to Frank.

"A light in the wood?" he asked. "Yes, it has appeared there several times. Just for a moment and then disappearing again. Some farmer, perhaps, finding his way home."

That was a very sensible conclusion, and for some reason that I did not trouble to probe my mind hastened to adopt it. After all, who was more likely to be passing through the wood than men from the upland farm going home at closing time from the Red Lion at St Caradoc's?

I was roused next morning out of very deep sleep by the entry of Mrs Fennell with hot water; it was a struggle to join myself up with the waking world again. I had the impression of having dreamed very vividly of things dark and dim, and of perilous places, and though I had certainly slept for something like eight hours at a stretch, I felt curiously unrefreshed. At breakfast Frank was more silent than his wont, but presently we were making plans for the day. He proposed to explore the wood again, while I was busy with my work; in the afternoon a round of golf would bring us to teatime. Before he started, and I settled down, we strolled about the garden that dozed tranquilly in the hot morning sun, and again congratulated ourselves on our exchange from the hotel. We went down to the pool below the quarried cliff, and there I left him to return to the house, while he, in order to start exploring at once, followed an overgrown path that led into the copse of birch and hornbeam of which I have spoken. But I had not crossed the lawn before I heard myself called.

"Come here a minute," he shouted, "I've found something interesting." I retraced my steps, and pushing through the trees found him standing by a tall, black granite stone that pushed its moss-green head above the undergrowth.

"It's a monolith," he said excitedly. "It's like one of those stones in the circle. Perhaps there has been another circle here, or, perhaps, it's a stone of the temple. It's deep in the earth, it looks as if it was in place. Let's see if we can find another in this copse."

He pushed on into the thick growing trees to the right of the path, and I, infected with his enthusiasm, made an exploration to the left. Before long I came upon another stone of the same character as the first, and my shout of discovery was echoed by his. Yet another rewarded his hunting, and as I emerged from the copse on the edge of the quarry pool I found a fifth one standing, but fallen forward in a bed of rushes that fringed the water.

In the excitement of this find, my planned studiousness was, of course, abandoned; so, too, when we had eaten a hearty lunch, was the projected game of golf, and before evening we had arrived at a rough scheme of the entire place. Most of the stones were in the belt of copse that half-encircled the house, and with a tape-measure we found that these were set at equal intervals from each other, except that exactly twice that interval separated the two stones that lay due east of the circle. In the bank that lay to the south of the house several were missing, but in each case, by digging at the proper intervals, we found fragments of granite grassed over in the soil, which indicated that these stones had been broken up and used, probably, for building materials, and this conjecture of Frank's was confirmed by the discovery of pieces of granite built into the walls of the house we occupied.

He had jotted down the approximate position of the stones, and passed over to me the paper on which he had drawn his plan.

"Without doubt it's a temple," he said, "there's the double interval at the east, which I told you about, and which was the gate into it."

I looked at what he had drawn.

"Then our house stands just in the centre of it," I said.

"Yes; what vandals they were to build it just there," said he. "Probably the stone of sacrifice lies somewhere below it. Good Lord, dinner ready, Mrs Fennell? I had no idea it was so late."

The sky had clouded over during the afternoon, and while we sat at dinner, a windless and heavy rain began to fall, and thunder to mutter over the sea. Mrs Fennell came in to enquire into our tastes for tomorrow, and as there was every appearance of a violent storm approaching, I asked her whether she and her girl would not stop here for the night and save themselves a wetting.

"No, I'll be off now, sir, thank you," she said. "We don't mind a wetting in Cornwall."

"But not very good for your rheumatism," I said. She had mentioned that she was a sufferer in this respect.

A blink of lightning flashed rather vividly across the uncurtained windows, and the rain hissed more heavily.

"No, I'll be off now," she said, "for it's late already. Good-night, gentlemen."

We heard her turn the key in the kitchen door, and presently the figures of herself and her girl passed the window.

"Not even umbrellas," said Frank. "They'll be drenched before they get down."

"I wonder why they wouldn't stop," said I.

Frank was soon employed on preparations for a plan to scale that he was meaning to make tomorrow, and he began putting in the house, which he had ascertained stood just in the centre of the temple. The size of the ground plan of it was all he required on the scale he intended for the complete plan, and after measuring the sitting-room, passage, and dining-room, he went through into the kitchen. Meanwhile, I had settled down to the work I had intended to do this morning, and purposed to get a couple of solid hours at it before I went to bed.

It was rather hard to get the thread of it again, and for some time I floundered with false starts and erased sentences, but before long I got into better form, and was already happily absorbed in it, when he called me from the kitchen.

"Oh, I can't come," I said, "I'm busy."

"Just a moment, please," he shouted.

I laid down my pen and went to him. He had moved the kitchen table aside and turned up the drugget that covered the floor.

"Look there!" he said.

The floor was paved with stone of the district, very likely from the quarry just outside. But in the centre was an oblong slab of black granite, some six feet by four in dimensions.

"That's a whacking big stone," I said. "Odd of them to have been at the trouble of putting that there."

"They didn't," said he. "I'll bet it was there when they laid the floor!"

Then I understood.

"The stone of sacrifice?" I asked.

"Rather. Black granite, and just in the centre of the temple. It can't be anything else."

Some sudden thrill of horror seized me. It was on that stone that young boys and maidens, torn from their mothers' arms, and bound hand and foot were laid, while the priest, with one hand over the victim's eyes, plunged the flint knife into the smooth, white throat, sawing through the tissue till the blood spurted from the severed artery... In the flickering light of the candle Frank carried, the stone seemed wet and darkly glistening, and was that noise only the rain volleying on the roof, or the beating of drums to drown the cries of the victim?...

"It's terrible," I said. "I wish you hadn't found it."

Frank was on his knees by it, examining the surface of it. "I can't say I agree with you," he said. "It just puts the final touch of certainty on my discovery. Besides, whether I had found it or not it would have been there just the same."

"Well, I'm going on with my work," I said. "It's more cheerful than stones of sacrifice."

He laughed.

"I hope it's as interesting," he said.

It appeared, when I went back to it, that it was not, and try as I would I could not recapture the interest which is necessary to production of any kind. Even my eye wandered from the words I wrote; as for my mind, it would give only the most cursory glance at that for which I demanded its fixed attention. It was busy elsewhere. I found myself, at its bidding, scrutinising the shadowy corners of the room, but there was nothing there, and all the time some strange darkness, blacker than that which pressed in upon the house, began to grow upon my spirit. There was fear mingled with it, though I did not know what I was afraid of, but chiefly it was some sort of despair and depression, distant as yet and undefined, but quietly closing in upon me... As I sat with my pen still in my hand, trying to analyse these perturbed and troubled sensations, I heard Frank call out sharply from the kitchen, the door of which, on my return, I had left open.

"Hullo!" he cried. "What's that? Is anyone there?"

I jumped from my seat and went to join him. He was standing close to the stove, holding his candle above his head, and looking at the door into the garden, which Mrs Fennell had locked on her departure.

"What's the matter?" I asked.

He looked round at me, startled by the sound of my voice.

"Curious," he said, "I was just measuring the stone, when out of the corner of my eye, I thought I saw that door open. But it's locked, isn't it?"

He tried the handle, but sure enough, it was locked.

"Optical delusion," he said. "Well, I've finished here for the present. But what a night! Frightfully oppressive, isn't it? And not a breath of air stirring."

We went back to the sitting-room. I put away my laboured manuscript and we got out the cards for a game of piquet. But after one *partie*, he rose with a yawn.

"I really don't think I could keep awake for another," he said, "I'm heavy with sleep. Let's have a breath of air, the rain seems to have stopped, and go to bed. Or are you going to sit up and work?"

I had not meant to do so, but his suggestion made me determine to have another try. There was certainly some mysterious pall of depression on me, and the wisest thing to do was to fight it.

"I shall try for half an hour," I said, "and see how it goes," and I followed him to the front door of the house. The rain, as he said, had ceased, but the darkness was impenetrable, and shuffling with our feet, we took a few steps along the gravel path to the corner of the house. There the light from the sitting-room windows cast a circle of illumination, and one could see the flower-beds glistening with the wet. Though it was night, the air was still so hot that the gravel path was steaming. Beyond that nothing was visible of the lawn or the hill that sloped up to the fir-wood. But, as we stood there, I saw, as last night, a light moving up there. Now, however, it seemed to be outside the wood, for its progress was not interrupted by the tree-trunks.

Frank saw it too, and pointed at it.

"It's too wet tonight," he said, "but tomorrow evening, I vote we go up there, and see who these nightly wanderers are. It's coming closer, and there's another of them."

Even as we looked a third light sprang up, and in another moment all had vanished again.

I carried out my intention of trying to work, but I could make nothing of it, and presently I found myself nodding over a page that contained nothing but erasures. With head bent forward, I drifted into a doze and from dozing into sleep, and when I woke I found the lamp burning low, and the wick smouldering. I seemed to have come back from some very distant place, and, only half awake, I lit a candle and quenched the lamp and went to the windows to bolt them. And then my heart stood still, for I thought I saw someone standing outside, and looking in through the intervening glass. But it must have been a sleepy fancy, for now, broad awake again, I was staring at my own reflection cast by the candle on the window. I told myself that what I had seen was no more than that, but as I creaked my way upstairs, I found myself asking if I really believed that...

As I dressed next morning, after another long but unrefreshed night, I began puzzling over a lost memory to which I had tried to find the clue yesterday. There was a bookcase in the sitting-room with some two or three dozen volumes in it, and opening one or two of these, I had found the name Samuel Townwick inscribed in them. I knew I had seen that name not so many months ago, in the daily Press, but I could not recapture the connection in which I had read it; but from the recurrence of it in these books, it was reasonable to conjecture that he was the owner of the house we occupied. In taking it, his name had not come up; the house agent had plenary powers, and our deposit of a fortnight's rent clinched the contract. But this morning the name still haunted me, and since I had other small businesses in St Caradoc's, I settled to walk down there and make some definite inquiry at the agent's. Frank was too busy with his plan to accompany me, and I set out alone.

The feeling of depression and vague foreboding was more leaden than ever this morning, and I was aware by that sixth sense, which needs not speech or language, that he was a prey to the same causeless weight. But I had not gone fifty yards from the house when the burden of it was lifted from me, and I knew again the exhilaration proper to such a morning. The rain of last evening had cleared the air, the sea breeze drew lightly landwards, and, as if I had come out of some tunnel, I rejoiced in the morning splendour. The village hummed with holiday: Mr Cranston received me with polite enquiries as to our comfort and Mrs Fennell's capability, and having assured him on that score, I approached my point.

"Mr Samuel Townwick is the owner, is he not?" I asked.

The agent's smile faded a little.

"He was, sir," he said. "I act for the executors."

Suddenly, in a flash, some of what I had been groping for came back to me. "I begin to remember," I said. "He died suddenly; there was an inquest. I want to know the rest. Hadn't you better tell me?"

He shifted his glance and came back to me again.

"It was a painful affair," he said. "The executors naturally do not want it talked about."

Another glimpse of what I had forgotten blinked on my memory.

"Suicide," I said. "The usual verdict of unsound mind was brought in. And—and is that why Mrs Fennell won't sleep in the house? She left last night in a deluge of rain."

I readily gave him my promise of secrecy, for I had not the slightest desire to tell Frank, and he told me the rest. Mr Townwick had been for some days in a very depressed state of mind, and one morning the servants coming down had found him lying underneath the kitchen table with his throat cut. Beside him was a sharp, curiously-shaped fragment of flint covered with blood. The jagged nature of the wound had confirmed the idea that he had sawn at his throat till he had severed the jugular vein. Murder was ruled out, for he was a strong man, and there were no marks on his body or about the room of there having been any struggle, nor any sign of an assailant having entered. Both kitchen doors were locked on the inside, his valuables were untouched, and from the position of the body the only reasonable inference was that he had laid down under the table, and there deliberately done himself to death… I repeated my assurance of silence and went out.

I knew now what the source of my nameless horror and depression had been. It was no haunting spectre of Townwick that I feared; it was the power, whatever that was, which had driven him to kill himself on the stone of sacrifice.

I went back up the hill: there was the garden blazing in the July noon, and the sweet tranquillity of the place was spread abroad in the air. But I had no sooner passed the copse and come within the circle than the dead weight of something unseen began to lay its burden on me again. There *was* something here, horrible and menacing and potent.

I found Frank in the sitting-room. His head was bent over his plan, and he started as I entered.

"Hullo!" he said. "I've made all my measurements and I want to sit tight and finish my plan today. I don't know why, but I feel I must hurry about it and get it done. And I've got the most awful fit of the blues. I can't account for it, but anyhow, occupation is the best thing. Go into lunch, will you, I don't want any."

I looked at him and saw some indefinable change had come over his face. There was terror in his eyes that came from within; I can express it in no other way than that.

"Anything wrong?" I asked.

"No; just blues. I want to go on working. This evening, you know, we have to see where those lights come from."

All afternoon he sat close over his work, and it was not till the day was failing that he got up.

"That's done," he said. "Good Lord, we have found a temple and a half! And I'm horribly tired. I shall have a snooze till dinner."

The invasion of fear beleaguered me, it seemed to pour in through the open windows in the gathering dusk, it gathered its reinforcements outside, ready to support the onrush of it. And yet how childish it was to yield to it. By now we were alone in the house, for we had told Mrs Fennell that a cold meal would serve us in this heat, and while Frank slept I had heard the lock of the outside kitchen door turn and she and the girl went by the window.

Presently he stirred and awoke. I had lit the lamp, and I saw his hand feel in his waistcoat pocket, and he drew out a small object which he held out to me.

"A flint knife," he said. "I picked it up in the garden this morning. It's got a fine edge to it."

At that I felt a prickle of terror run through the hair of my head, and I jumped up.

"Look here," I said, "you've had no walk today, and that always gives you the blues. Let's go down and dine at the hotel."

His head was outside the illumination of the lamp, and from the dimness there came a curious cackle of laughter.

"But I can't," he said. "How strange that you don't know that I can't. They've surrounded the place, and there's no way out. Listen! Can't you hear the drums and the squeal of their fifes? And their hands are about me. Christ! It's terrible to die."

He got up and began to move with curious little shuffling steps towards the kitchen. I had laid the flint knife down on the table, and he snatched it up. The horror of presences unseen and multitudinous closed in round me, but I knew they were concentrated not on me, but on him. They poured in not through the window alone, but through the solid walls of the house; outside on the lawn there were lights moving, slow and orderly.

I had still control of my mind; the awfulness and the imminence of what so closely beset us gave me the courage and clearness of despair. I darted from my chair and stood with my back to the kitchen door.

"You're not to go in there," I said. "You must come away with me out of this. Pull yourself together, Frank. We'll get through yet; once across the garden we're safe."

He paid no attention to what I said; it was as if he did not hear me. He laid his hand on my shoulder, and I felt his fingers press through the muscles and grind like points of steel on the underlying bone. Some maniac force possessed them, and he pulled me aside as if I had been a feather.

There was one thing only to be done. With my disengaged arm I hit him full on the chin, and he fell like a log across the floor. Without pausing for a second I gripped him round the knees and began dragging him senseless and inert towards the door...

It is difficult to state in words what those next few minutes held. I saw nothing. I heard nothing. I felt no touch of invisible hands upon me, but I can imagine no grinding agony of pain that wrenches body and soul asunder to equal that war of the evil and the unseen that raged about me. I struggled against no visible adversary, and there was the horror of it, for I am sure that no phantom of the dead that die not could have evoked so unnerving a terror.

Before those intangible hosts had fully closed in round me and my unconscious burden, I had got him on to the lawn, and it was then that the full stress of their beleaguering might poured in upon me. Strange fugitive lights wavered round me and muttered voices filled the air, and as I dragged Frank over the grass his weight seemed to grow till it was not a man's body that I was pulling along, but something well-nigh immovable, so that I had to tug and pant for breath and tug again.

"God help us both," I heard myself muttering. "Deliver us from our ghostly enemies..." and again I tugged and panted for breath. Close at hand now was the ring of enclosing copse, where the stones of the circle stood, and I made one final effort of concentration, for I knew that my spirit was spent, and soon there would be no power of fight left in me at all.

"In the name of the Holiest, and in the power of the Highest," I cried aloud, and waited for a moment, gathering what dregs of strength were still left in me. And then I leaned forward, and the strained sinews of my legs were slackened as the weight of Frank's body moved after me, and I made another step, and yet another, and we had passed beyond the copse, and out of the accursed precinct.

I knew no more after that. I had fallen forwards half across him, and when I regained my senses, he was stirring, and the dew of the grass was on my face. There stood the house, with the lamp still burning in the window of the sitting-room, and the quiet night was around us, with a clear and starry heaven.

# THE SPIRIT OF STONEHENGE

## *Jasper John*

Jasper John was the pseudonym of the British journalist Rosalie Muspratt (1906–1976), under which she published two collections of supernatural short stories, *Sinister Stories* (1930) and *Tales of Terror* (1931). While these were somewhat successful commercially, she didn't return to the theme in her writing again. Her interest in supernatural tales may have been piqued by the fact that she allegedly grew up in several haunted houses. Her story "The Spirit of Stonehenge" appeared in *Sinister Stories* and deals with Druid worship, elementals, and sacrifice.

"So you have moved from your old home; I was rather surprised to hear," I said to Ronald Dalton.

He nodded his head.

"We were very sorry to go, but nothing would have made us stay after what had happened. I know I did not tell you, but then we have not spoken of it more than is necessary, even to old friends."

We were sitting in the twilight of a June evening. Outside the rain dripped from the trees, from the roof, from the windows; for there had been a dreadful thunderstorm.

"I would like to tell you what happened, if you care to listen," Ronald said abruptly.

I had been rather hoping he would, for he was a matter-of-fact man, and my curiosity had been stirred by the papers' accounts of the strange way one of their guests had committed suicide. So he started in his earnest way, which lent conviction to the story.

"My brother made great friends with Gavin Thomson in London. The first time I saw him was when he came to stay with us for a week. His great hobby was to dabble about in excavations, and, as his father had left him enough to live comfortably, he was able to indulge his taste.

"He was a good-looking boy, about twenty-nine, dark and manly. Though only young, he had made quite a name for himself already, even with the professors. There were tales of his living among the Bedouins, an unheard-of thing for a white man to do. But it was difficult to make him talk of his exploits.

47

"I took to him, as my brother had done; he had such a magnetic personality. He told us he had been reading up all the old books on Stonehenge which he could get hold of. The Druid theory fascinated him, and he was anxious to study some facts first-hand.

"He asked us if we had ever heard of elementals; then laughed, and said we were not to be afraid that *he* was possessed by them. We asked him what the things were, for beneath his light manner I saw that he was really serious about them. He told us that they were a sort of ugly evil spirits, which had never had a form. Their one object was to find a human body in which to reside. They were supposed to have a certain power over human beings in places where great evil had prevailed.

"Quite abruptly he stopped, and began talking about the moon's rays on the dolmen at Stonehenge, and a peculiar theory he held, of which we understood nothing. I think he meant to puzzle us and make us forget.

"Now and then he descended to our level when he explained that the Druids were fond of conducting their ceremonies at certain times of the moon. 'That is why I have to do so much of my work at night,' he said. We had given him a latchkey so that he could come in when he liked. He told us that he was on the verge of a great discovery which would make history.

"After a fortnight's stay he left us to do some work in Brittany, but not before he had covered many sheets with writing. In three months he was back again. He looked gaunt and ill, and his eyes were sunken and bright with fever. We begged him to rest that night, but he would not hear of it, and when he spoke of Stonehenge his eyes gleamed in a strange manner.

"When he had gone out into the night I went up to his room to see if there was everything that he could want. There were books everywhere; one lay on the table, the place was marked with something. I opened it at the place and a knife lay snugly between the pages. It was curved, and of pure gold. I knew enough to know that it was a copy of a sacrificial knife; the edge was so sharp that I cut my finger rather badly.

"Curiosity aroused, I looked at the page, and this is what I read:

> "'ELEMENTALS OF STONEHENGE. Though the day of the Druids is now long passed and the cries of their victims no longer haunt the night and the altar stone has ceased to drip blood, yet it is dangerous to go there when the sacrificial moon is full. For the Druids, by the blood they shed, their vile sacrifices and fellowship with the devil, attracted forces of evil to the place. So it is said that shapeless invisible horrors haunt the vicinity and at certain times crave a resting place in a human body. If once they enter in, it is only with difficulty that they are evicted.'

"The book was many centuries old. I looked at the other books; they were all on the same subject. Gavin seemed to be quite crazy about it. I told my brother, and he said that he thought poor Gavin was overstrung.

"'Perhaps he is possessed by an elemental,' he said, and we both laughed.

"Next night we resolved to follow him. When he went out as usual, the dog, to our surprise, jumped into the car. Gavin threw him out with a force that surprised us, and bade us call him back. We endeavoured to do so, but the animal seemed demented; he ran after the car like a mad thing, and both were soon lost in the distance.

"After half an hour we followed on the same road. It was a lovely night, warm, with the sky full of scudding clouds which every now and then hid the face of the moon and dimmed its light. Some little way off we left the car and started to walk across the grass. Tall and gaunt the dolmen stood out where the moonlight touched them. Somehow, to me they looked unaccountably sinister, as if they longed to fall and crush one.

"We were still some way off when we saw a figure steal out from one of the great stones. In the dim light it looked like a misty wraith. I heard my brother draw in his breath sharply.

"It stopped before the altar stone, which was deeply in the shadow. Something flashed in the light—a knife; then it seemed from the stone itself came the most ear-splitting howl of agony.

"The moon went behind a cloud; we fled, stumbling over the wet grass, and in our haste missed the car. At last we found it, and, tumbling in, drove off at a great pace. When we got back again Gavin was already in bed and had to come down to open the door. He was too tired to notice anything wrong, and we just said that we had been for a drive.

"Next day, after rather a sleepless night, we were heartily ashamed of our weakness, and firmly resolved to follow Gavin again that night. All day he seemed very absorbed and dreamy, and talked only about the discovery that he was going to make.

"An hour after he had left we were on his track. This time there was no moon, but we had an electric torch. I soon caught sight of Gavin; he was kneeling by the altar stone. It was reassuring to see his tweed-clad figure. We came up right behind, but he did not turn his head. Then I put my hand on his shoulder, but he did not move. He was unconscious. I raised his head and the light fell on glazed eyes, for he was dead. We laid him on the altar stone seeking for a spark of life, but all in vain. There was blood on his shirt and the hilt of a little knife stuck out. There he lay on the sacrificial stone with hair dishevelled, white upturned face and glassy eyes, while above towered the great stones, seeming to rejoice that once again homage had been paid by a sacrifice of blood. Queer shadows danced in the light of the lamp which my brother held in shaking hands.

"We stood with bowed heads in the presence of those great monuments; tombstones that would have done honour to a king. Then we gathered courage and took the body to the car. And Stonehenge let us go, content that once again its stones were wet with blood.

"It was an unconsidered thing we did, in that, and it might have led us into trouble; but we found a letter written by Gavin and his will which he had made, so we were freed from all blame or share in the matter.

"He said that the first few nights of his excavations at Stonehenge he had been unassailed and in a perfectly normal state of mind. Then a strange change came over him, so that at times he almost seemed to have lived there years before and to know all manner of secrets.

"Then it was that the desire to do the most dreadful things came over him. He questioned if he were mad or if it was the spirit of Stonehenge demanding a victim. The idea of elementals occurred to him, for he had been reading much about them of late.

"At last he tore himself away and went to Brittany to bury himself in work. But Stonehenge called him back, and he seemed to lose all power over himself. At last, after many sleepless nights, he came back, as he had known that he must.

"Then, one night he had seen a dog lying on the altar stone, and a irresistible desire to kill overpowered him. After the blood was shed he felt a strange joy and deep contentment, but something told him that he was being watched, so he took the body and ran to the car. He had discovered a short cut across the grass which cut off many miles, so that was how he got home before us.

"Next morning he awoke with the blood lust strong within him; he felt that if anything would come upon him at the Stones he must kill. All day he fought it. At times he would be filled with disgust at his thoughts, then fall to devising a plot to lure us to our fate.

"When we had mentioned our coming, a cold fear had seized him, but his words died in his throat when he tried to warn us. Then all the good that was in him seemed to make one last stand. He knew there was one way out—to offer a sacrifice of blood, and the victim to be himself.

"So that night he had offered his life as a propitiation for evil in the hope that he would regain the soul that once was his. He ended by begging us to forgive and forget.

"The letter accomplished a purpose. 'Suicide while of unsound mind,' was brought in. Suspicion was lifted from us, but afterwards Bob and I went away from the horrible place."

No one spoke. We sat in dead silence when he had finished. Then the gong rang, and we arose and knocked the ashes from our pipes.

# THE FIRST SHEAF

## H. R. Wakefield

Herbert Russell Wakefield (1888–1964) was an Oxford graduate, a WWI veteran, publisher, and civil servant. It was towards the end of the 1920s that he began to write ghost stories, publishing the acclaimed collection *They Return at Evening* in 1928. He continued to publish collections of both ghost and mystery fiction, as well non-fiction crime studies, alongside short stories in magazines such as *Weird Tales* until his death. For a time, he was highly acclaimed, John Betjeman stating that "M. R. James is the greatest master of the ghost story. Henry James, Sheridan Le Fanu and H. Russell Wakefield are equal seconds." Wakefield believed in the supernatural; as he himself stated in his essay "Why I Write Ghost Stories" from the 1940 collection *The Clock Strikes Twelve*, he had "experienced them [psychic phenomena] myself". As such, he believed in the factual possibility of all the tales he wrote.

The story here, also published in *The Clock Strikes Twelve*, is an unusual variant from Wakefield's normal ghost stories, and could well be regarded as an early example of the folk horror genre, with its tale of a small rural village, its unwelcoming inhabitants, and pagan harvest rituals.

"If only they realised what they were doing!" laughed old Porteous, leaning over the side of the car. "They" were a clutter of rustics, cuddling vegetable marrows, cauliflowers, apples, and other stuffs, passing into a village church some miles south of Birmingham. "Humanity has been doing that, performing that rite, since thousands of years before the first syllable of recorded time, I suppose; though not always in quite such a refined manner. And then there are maypoles, of all indecorous symbols, and beating the bounds, a particularly interesting survival with, originally, a dual function; first they beat the bounds to scare the devils out, and then they beat the small boys that their tears might propitiate the Rain Goddess. Such propitiation having been found to be superfluous in this climate, they have ceased to beat the urchins; a great pity, but an admirable example of myth-adaptation. Great Britain swarms with such survivals, some as innocuous and bland as this harvest festival, others far more formidable and guarded secrets; at least that was so when I was a boy. Did I ever tell you how I lost my arm?"

"No," I replied, yawning. "Go ahead. But I hope the tale has entertainment value, for I am feeling deliciously sleepy."

Old Porteous leaned back and lit a cigar. He had started his career with fifty pounds, and turned this into seven figures by sheer speculative genius; he seemed to touch nothing which did not appreciate. He is fat, shrewd, cynical, and very charitable in an individual, far-sighted way. A copious but discriminating eater and drinker, to all appearances just a superb epitome of a type. But he has a less mundane side which is highly developed, being a devoted amateur of music with a trained and individual taste. And he owns the finest collection of keyboard instruments in Europe, the only one of his many possessions I very greatly envy him. Music, indeed, was the cause of our being together that Sunday morning in August, for I make my living out of attempting to criticise it, and we were driving to Manchester for a Harty Sibelius concert.

When I was a boy of thirteen [he began] my father accepted the living of Reedley End in Essex. There was little competition for the curé as the place had a notable reputation for toughness in the diocese, and the stipend was two hundred and fifty pounds a year and a house which, in size and amenities, somewhat resembled a contemporary poor-house. However, the prospect appealed to my dear old dad's zeal, for he was an Evangelist by label and temperament.

Reedley End was in one of those remote corners of the country which are "backwaterish" to this day; and was then almost as cut off from the world as a village in Tibet. It sprawled along the lower slopes of a short, narrow valley, was fifteen miles from a railway station, and its only avenue to anywhere was a glorified cart-track. It was peopled by a strange tribe, aloof, dour, bitter, and revealing copious signs of intensive interbreeding. They greeted my father's arrival with contemptuous nonchalance, spurned his ministrations, and soon enough broke his spirit.

"I can do nothing with them!" he groaned, half to himself and half to me. "They seem to worship other gods than mine!"

There was a very real justification for their bitterness. Reedley End was, perhaps, the most arid spot in Britain; drought, save in very good years, was endemic in that part of Essex, and I believe a bad spring and dry summer still causes great inconvenience and some hardship to this day. There had been three successive drought years before our arrival, with crop failures, heavy mortality amongst the beasts, and actual thirst the result. The distress was great and growing, and a mood of venomous despair had come with it. There was no one to help them—the day of Governmental paternalism had not yet dawned, and my father's predecessor's prayers for rain had been a singularly ineffectual substitute. They were off the map and left to stew in their own juice—or rather perish from the lack of it. Men in such a pass, if they cannot look forward for succour, many times look back.

In February they went forth to sow again, and my father told me they seemed to him in a sinister and enigmatic mood. (I may say my mother had died five years before, I was an only child, and through being my father's confidant, was old and "wise" for my age.) Their habitual aloofness had become impenetrable, and all—even the children—seemed imbued with some communal purpose, sharers of some communal secret.

One morning my father went to visit an ancient, bedridden crone who snubbed him with less consistent ruthlessness than the rest of his fearsome flock. To his astonishment he found the village entirely deserted. When he entered the ancient's cottage she abruptly told him to be gone.

"It is no day for you to be abroad, parson," she said peremptorily. "Go home and stay indoors!"

In his bewilderment my father attempted to solve the humiliating mystery, and decided to visit one of the three small farmers who strove desperately to scrape a living for themselves and their hinds from the parched acres; and who had treated him with rough courtesy. His farmhouse was some two miles away and my father set out to walk there. But, on reaching the outskirts of the village, he found his way barred by three men placed like sentries across the track. They waved him back without a word, and when he made some show of passing them, grew so threatening and their gestures so unmistakable, that my father cut short his protests and came miserably home again.

That night I couldn't sleep; my father's disturbed mood had communicated itself to me. Some time in the course of it I went to my window and leaned out. A bitter northerly wind was blowing, and suddenly down it came a horrid, thin cry of agony that seemed to have been carried from afar. It came once again, diminished and cut short. I crept shivering and badly scared back to bed.

If my father had heard it he made no reference to it next morning, when the village seemed itself again. And though the children were brooding and subdued, their elders were almost in good spirits, ruthlessly jocund, like homing lynchers. (I made that comparison, of course, long afterwards, but I know it to be psychologically true.)

My father had made valiant and pathetic attempts to get hold of the village youth and managed to coax together a meagre attendance at a Sunday school. On the next Sunday one of the dozen was missing. This was a girl of about my own age, the only child of a farm-labourer and his wife. He was a "foreigner", a native of Sussex, and a sparklingly handsome fellow of the pure Saxon type. His wife had some claims to be a beauty, too, and was much fairer than the average of those parts. The result was an oddly lovely child, as fair and rosy as her father. She shone out in the village like a Golden Oriole in a crew of crows. She aroused my keenest curiosity, the bud of love, I suppose; and I spent much of my time spying on her from a shy distance. When she failed to turn up that Sunday, my father went round to her parents' cottage. They were both at home. The man was pacing up and down the kitchen, his face revealing fury and grief. The mother was sitting in front of the fire, wearing an expression my father found it hard to analyse. It reminded him of the appearance often shown by religious maniacs in their less boisterous moments; ecstatic, exalted, yet essentially unbalanced. When he asked after the little girl, the father clenched his fists and swore fiercely; the woman, without turning her head, muttered, "She'll be coming to school no more." This ultimatum was naturally not good enough for my father, who was disagreeably affected by the scene. He asked where she was. She'd been sent away. "Where to?" he asked. But at this she became a raging virago and ordered my father to go and mind his own business. He turned to the man, who seemed on the verge of an outburst, but she muttered something my father couldn't catch and he ran from the room.

Late that night my dad heard a tap on his study window. It was the father.

"Sir," he said, "I'm away. They're devils here!"

"Your little girl?" asked my father, horrified.

"They've taken her," he replied hoarsely. "I don't know why, and I don't know where she's gone. But I know I shan't see her no more. As for my wife, I hate her for what she's done. She says they'll kill me if I try to find her. They'd kill me if they knew I was here!"

My father implored him to tell him more; promised him sanctuary and protection, but all he said was, "Avenge her, sir!" and vanished into the night.

Naturally my father was at a loss what to do. He even enlisted my more than willing aid. But all I succeeded in doing was verifying the agonising fact that my darling had gone, and taking a terrific beating from persons unknown one night when I was snooping near the cottage.

In the end my father wrote a confidential letter to the Colchester police outlining the circumstances. But I suppose his tale was so vague and discreet that, though some enquiries were made by a thick-skulled, pot-bellied constable, nothing whatsoever came of them. But my father was a marked man from the moment of this peeler's appearance, and audible and impertinent interruptions punctuated his services.

Realising he was beaten, he made up his mind, with many tears and self-reproaches, to resign at the end of the year.

The week after the little girl's disappearance there was a lovely two days' rain, and the spring and summer were a farmer's Elysian dream. My father, with pathetic optimism, hoped this copious, if belated, answer to his prayers would improve his status with his iron-fleeced flock. Instead he experienced a unanimous and shattering ostracism. In despair he wrote to his bishop, but the episcopal counsel was couched in too general and booming terms to be efficacious in converting the denizens of Reedley End.

And one day it was August, the fields shone with a mighty harvest, and it was time to bring it home.

The valley divided the corn-lands of Reedley into two areas tilled against the slight slopes. Those facing north were noticeably less productive than those on the south and do not concern us. Those southern fields were open and treeless, with one exception, a comparatively small circular field in the very middle of the tilled expanse. This was completely hemmed in by evergreens, yews, and holm-oaks; not a single deciduous tree interrupted the dark barrier. In the centre of this field was a stone pillar about eight feet high. I was forced to be by myself for many hours a day; and I spent many of them roaming the countryside and peopling it with the folk of my fancy. The local youth regarded me without enthusiasm, but young blood is thicker than old and they did not keep me in rigid "Coventry", though they were very guarded in their replies to my questions.

This circular field stirred an intense curiosity within me, and all my wanderings on the southern slopes seemed to bring me, sooner or later, to its boundaries. Eventually I summoned up courage to ask a lad who had shown traces of cordiality if the field had a name—for some reason I was sure it had. He looked at me oddly—nervously and angrily—and replied, "It's the Good Field; and nought to do with you!" After the little girl's disappearance I was convinced, vaguely but certainly, that this field was concerned with it; intuition I suppose.

"Now that," I interrupted, "is a word that baffles me; and the dictionary seems to know no more than I do."

In a way I agree [laughed old Porteous], I could answer you negatively and quite accurately by saying that it is a mode of apprehension unknown to women. But I believe an intuitive judgment to be a syllogism of which the premises are in the Unconscious, the conclusion in the Conscious, though retrospective meditation can sometimes resolve it into a normal thought process. I have often done so in the case of big deals. It is the speed of the intuitive process which is so valuable. And now I hope you are a wiser man!

Anyway I conceived a fascinated horror of the field, a shivering curiosity concerning it I longed to satisfy.

One evening, early in March, I determined to do what I had never dared before, walk out into the field and examine the stone pillar. It was almost dusk and not a soul in sight. When I'd surmounted a small but deep ditch, broken through between two yews, and stood out in that strange place under a hurrying, unstable sky, I felt a sense of extreme isolation; not, I think, the isolation of being alone in a deserted place, but such as one would experience if alone and horribly conspicuous amongst a hostile crowd. However, I fought down my fears and strode forward. When I reached the pillar I found it was square and surrounded by a small, cleared expanse of neatly tiled stone. This stone was thickly stained with what appeared to be red rust. The pillar itself was heavily pitted and indented about a third from its top, with such regularity as suggested an almost obliterated inscription of some kind. I clasped the pillar with my arms, tucked my legs round it, and heaved myself up till I could touch its top. This I found to be hollowed out into a cup. I stretched up farther and pushed my fingers down. The next moment I was lying on my back and wringing my fingers; for if I had dipped my hand into molten lead I couldn't have known a sharper scald. This emptied my little bag of courage and, with "zero at the bone", I got up and ran for it. As I stumbled forward I took one look over my shoulder, and it seemed to me there was a dark figure standing by the pillar and reaching high above its top; and all the time I gasped homewards I felt I had a follower, and the pursuit was not called off till I flung myself through the rectory door.

"What's the matter?" asked my father. "You shouldn't run like that. And you've cut your hand. Go and bathe it."

They started to reap in the second week of August and I found the process of great interest, for it was the first harvest I had seen. I hovered about the outskirts of the activity, fearing my reception if I ventured nearer. I found they were working in towards the Round Field from all points of the compass; and, young and inexperienced as I was, it seemed to me the people were in a strange mood, or rather mood-cycle, for at times there would be outbursts of wild singing, with horse-play and gesticulation, and at others they would be even more morose and silent than had been their sombre wont. And day after day they drew nearer the Round Field.

They reached it from all sides almost simultaneously by about noon on a superbly fine day. And then to my astonishment, they all stopped work and went home. That was on a Tuesday, and they did nothing the next day in the fields, though they were anything but idle. There was incessant activity in the village of a sort which perplexed my father greatly. It struck him that something of great importance was being prepared. The hive was seething. Needless to say no knowledge of it was vouchsafed to him. He discovered by humiliating experience that a meeting of the older men was held in what was known as "Odiues Field", for the sentries posted round all the approaches to it brusquely and menacingly refused him entrance.

Now whether it was our old friend, Intuition, or not, I was convinced these plans and consultations concerned the Round Field, and that something was due to be done there on the morrow. So I crept out of the house an hour before dawn, leaving a note on the hall-table telling my father not to worry. I took with me three slices of bread-and-butter and a bottle of water. I made my way to the Round Field by a devious route so as to avoid passing through the village, creeping along the hedgerows and keeping a sharp look-out with eye and ear. I have said that a ditch encircled the field, and in it I crouched down between two yews, well away from the gates. By creeping into the space where their branches touched, I believed I could spy out undetected.

Dawn broke fine, but very heavy and close, and there were red strata of clouds to the east as the sun climbed through them.

To my surprise no one appeared at six, their usual hour for starting work, nor at seven, eight, or nine, when I ate half my bread-and-butter and sipped the bottle. By ten o'clock I had made up my mind that nothing would happen and I'd better go home, when I heard voices in the field behind me and knew it was too late to retreat if I'd wanted to. I could see nothing ahead of me save the high, white wheat, but presently I heard more voices and two men with sickles came cutting their way past me, and soon I could see an arc of a ring of them slashing towards the centre. When they had advanced some fifty yards I had a better view to right and left, and a very strange sight I beheld. The villagers, mostly old people and children, were streaming through the gates. All were clad in black with wreaths of corn around their necks. They formed in line behind the reapers and moved slowly forward. They made no sound—I heard not a single child's cry—but stared in a rapt way straight before them. Slowly and steadily the reapers cut their way forward. By this time the sun had disappeared and a dense cloud-bank was spreading from the east. By four o'clock the reapers had met in the centre round the last small patch of wheat by the stone pillar. And there they stopped, laid down their sickles, and took their stand in front of the people. For, perhaps, five minutes they all stayed motionless with bowed heads. And then they lifted their faces to the sky and began to chant. And a very odd song they sang, one which made me shiver beneath the yew branches. It was mainly in the minor mode, but at perfectly regular intervals it transposed into the major in a tremendous, but perfectly controlled, cry of exaltation and ecstasy. I have heard nothing like it since, though a "Spiritual", sung by four thousand god-drunk chanters in Georgia, faintly reminded me of it. But this was something far more formidable, far more primitive; in fact it seemed like the oldest song ever sung. The last, fierce, sustained shout of triumph made me tremble with some unnameable emotion, and I longed to be out there shouting with them. When it ended they all knelt down save one old, white-bearded man with a wreath of corn around his brow who, taking some of the corn in his right hand, raised it above his head and stared into the sky. At once four men came forward and, with what seemed like large trowels, began digging with them. The people then rose to their feet, somewhat obstructing my view. But soon the four men had finished their work and stood upright. Then the old man stepped out again and I could see he was holding what appeared to be a short iron bar. With this he pounded the earth for some moments. Then, picking up something, it looked as if he dropped it into a vessel, a dark, metal pot, I fancied, and paced to the stone-pillar, raised his right arm, and poured the contents into the cup at the pillar's top. At that moment a terrific flash of lightning cut down from the clouds and enveloped the pillar in mauve and devilish flame; and there came such a piercing blast of thunder that I fell backwards into the ditch. When I'd struggled back, the rain was hurling itself down in such fury that it was bouncing high off the lanes of stiff soil. Dimly through it I could see that all the folk had prostrated themselves once more. But in two minutes the thunder-cloud had run with the squall and the sun was blazing from a clear sky. The four men then bound up the corn in that last patch and placed the sheaf in front of the pillar. After which the old man, leading the people, paced the length of the field, scattering something from the vessel in the manner of one sowing. And he led them out of the gate and that was the last I saw of them.

Now somehow I felt that if they knew I'd been watching them, it would have gone hard with me. So I determined to wait for dusk. I was stiff, cold, and hungry, but I stuck it till the sun went flaming down and the loveliest after-glow I ever remember had faded. While I waited there a resolve had been forming in my mind. I had the most intense desire to know what the old man had dropped in the hollow on the pillar, and curiosity is in all animals the strongest foe of fear. Every moment that emotion grew more compelling, and when at last it was just not dark it became over-mastering. I stumbled across as fast as I could to the pillar, looking neither to right nor left, clambered up, and thrust down my hand. I could feel small pieces of what might have been wood, and then it was as if my forefinger was caught and gripped. The most agonising pain shot up my arm and through my body. I fell to the ground and shook my hand wildly to free my finger from that which held it. In the end it clattered down beside me and splintered on the stone. And then the blood streamed from my finger, which had been punctured to the bone. Somehow I struggled home, leaving a trail of blood behind me.

The next day my arm was swollen up like a black bladder; the morning after it was amputated at the shoulder. The surgeon who operated on me came up to my father in the hospital and held something out to him. "I found this embedded in your son's finger," he said.

"What is it?" asked my father.

"A child's tooth," he replied. "I suppose he's been fighting someone, someone with a very dirty mouth!"

"And that's why," said old Porteous, "though I have none of my own, I have ever since shown the greatest respect to the gods of others."

# THE TARN OF SACRIFICE

## *Algernon Blackwood*

Algernon Blackwood (1869–1951) is one of the foremost names in weird fiction, his work formed by his personal experiences and interests in nature, the wilderness and mysticism. His first publication came in 1906, a collection of stories called *The Empty House and Other Ghost Stories*, and he continued to publish up until his death. His most famous work is probably "The Willows", published in 1907, which is informed with an animistic view of nature. Blackwood was fascinated by spiritualism and the occult, being at one point a member of the Hermetic Order of the Golden Dawn and interested in the work of the Society of Psychical Research, but his earlier interests were in Hinduism and esoteric Buddhism—which may be where his interest in the concept of reincarnation developed. This is a theme which appears in several of his works, both fiction and non-fiction, in particular in the novels *Julius LeVallon* and its sequel *The Bright Messenger*, and the un-performed play *Karma: A Reincarnation Play*, co-written with Violet Pearn. In his essay "On Reincarnation", he states his hope "that reincarnation is the true explanation of life and its inequalities on every plane". The story here, first published in *The Wolves of God and Other Fey Stories* in 1921, deals with themes of reincarnation, standing stones, and sacrifice.

John Holt, a vague excitement in him, stood at the door of the little inn, listening to the landlord's directions as to the best way of reaching Scarsdale. He was on a walking tour through the Lake District, exploring the smaller dales that lie away from the beaten track and are accessible only on foot.

The landlord, a hard-featured north countryman, half innkeeper, half sheep farmer, pointed up the valley. His deep voice had a friendly burr in it.

"You go straight on till you reach the head," he said, "then take to the fell. Follow the 'sheep-trod' past the Crag. Directly you're over the top you'll strike the road."

"A road up there!" exclaimed his customer incredulously.

"Aye," was the steady reply. "The old Roman road. The same road," he added, "the savages came down when they burst through the Wall and burnt everything right up to Lancaster—"

"They were held—weren't they—at Lancaster?" asked the other, yet not knowing quite why he asked it.

"I don't rightly know," came the answer slowly. "Some say they were. But the old town has been that built over since, it's hard to tell." He paused a moment. "At Ambleside," he went on presently, "you can still see the marks of the burning, and at the little fort on the way to Ravenglass."

Holt strained his eyes into the sunlit distance, for he would soon have to walk that road and he was anxious to be off. But the landlord was communicative and interesting. "You can't miss it," he told him. "It runs straight as a spear along the fell top till it meets the Wall. You must hold to it for about eight miles. Then you'll come to the Standing Stone on the left of the track—"

"The Standing Stone, yes?" broke in the other a little eagerly.

"You'll see the Stone right enough. It was where the Romans came. Then bear to the left down another 'trod' that comes into the road there. They say it was the war-trail of the folk that set up the Stone."

"And what did they use the Stone for?" Holt inquired, more as though he asked it of himself than of his companion.

The old man paused to reflect. He spoke at length.

"I mind an old fellow who seemed to know about such things called it a Sighting Stone. He reckoned the sun shone over it at dawn on the longest day right on to the little holm in Blood Tarn. He said they held sacrifices in a stone circle there." He stopped a moment to puff at his black pipe. "Maybe he was right. I have seen stones lying about that may well be that."

The man was pleased and willing to talk to so good a listener. Either he had not noticed the curious gesture the other made, or he read it as a sign of eagerness to start. The sun was warm, but a sharp wind from the bare hills went between them with a sighing sound. Holt buttoned his coat about him. "An odd name for a mountain lake—Blood Tarn," he remarked, watching the landlord's face expectantly.

"Aye, but a good one," was the measured reply. "When I was a boy the old folk had a tale that the savages flung three Roman captives from that crag into the water. There's a book been written about it; they say it was a sacrifice, but most likely they were tired of dragging them along, I say. Anyway, that's what the writer said. One, I mind, now you ask me, was a priest of some heathen temple that stood near the Wall, and the other two were his daughter and her lover." He guffawed. At least he made a strange noise in his throat. Evidently, thought Holt, he was sceptical yet superstitious. "It's just an old tale handed down, whatever the learned folk may say," the old man added.

"A lonely place," began Holt, aware that a fleeting touch of awe was added suddenly to his interest.

"Aye," said the other, "and a bad spot too. Every year the Crag takes its toll of sheep, and sometimes a man goes over in the mist. It's right beside the track and very slippery. Ninety foot of a drop before you hit the water. Best keep round the tarn and leave the Crag alone if there's any mist about. Fishing? Yes, there's some quite fair trout in the tarn, but it's not much fished. Happen one of the shepherd lads from Tyson's farm may give it a turn with an 'otter,'" he went on, "once in a while, but he won't stay for the evening. He'll clear out before sunset."

"Ah! Superstitious, I suppose?"

"It's a gloomy, chancy spot—and with the dusk falling," agreed the innkeeper eventually. "None of our folk care to be caught up there with night coming on. Most handy for a shepherd, too—but Tyson can't get a man to bide there." He paused again, then added significantly: "Strangers don't seem to mind it though. It's only our own folk—"

"Strangers!" repeated the other sharply, as though he had been waiting all along for this special bit of information. "You don't mean to say there are people living up there?" A curious thrill ran over him.

"Aye," replied the landlord, "but they're daft folk—a man and his daughter. They come every spring. It's early in the year yet, but I mind Jim Backhouse, one of Tyson's men, talking about them last week." He stopped to think. "So they've come back," he went on decidedly. "They get milk from the farm."

"And what on earth are they doing up there?" Holt asked.

He asked many other questions as well, but the answers were poor, the information not forthcoming. The landlord would talk for hours about the Crag, the tarn, the legends and the Romans, but concerning the two strangers he was uncommunicative. Either he knew little, or he did not want to discuss them; Holt felt it was probably the former. They were educated town-folk, he gathered with difficulty, rich apparently, and they spent their time wandering about the fell, or fishing. The man was often seen upon the Crag, his girl beside him, bare-legged, dressed as a peasant. "Happen they come for their health, happen the father is a learned man studying the Wall"—exact information was not forthcoming.

The landlord "minded his own business," and inhabitants were too few and far between for gossip. All Holt could extract amounted to this: the couple had been in a motor accident some years before, and as a result they came every spring to spend a month or two in absolute solitude, away from cities and the excitement of modern life. They troubled no one and no one troubled them.

"Perhaps I may see them as I go by the tarn," remarked the walker finally, making ready to go. He gave up questioning in despair. The morning hours were passing.

"Happen you may," was the reply, "for your track goes past their door and leads straight down to Scarsdale. The other way over the crag saves half a mile, but it's rough going along the scree." He stopped dead. Then he added, in reply to Holt's good-bye: "In my opinion it's not worth it," yet what he meant exactly by "it" was not quite clear.

The walker shouldered his knapsack. Instinctively he gave the little hitch to settle it on his shoulders—much as he used to give to his pack in France. The pain that shot through him as he did so was another reminder of France. The bullet he had stopped on the Somme still made its presence felt at times... Yet he knew, as he walked off briskly, that he was one of the lucky ones. How many of his old pals would never walk again, condemned to hobble on crutches for the rest of their lives! How many, again, would never even hobble! More terrible still, he remembered, were the blind... The dead, it seemed to him, had been more fortunate...

He swung up the narrowing valley at a good pace and was soon climbing the fell. It proved far steeper than it had appeared from the door of the inn, and he was glad enough to reach the top and fling himself down on the coarse springy turf to admire the view below.

The spring day was delicious. It stirred his blood. The world beneath looked young and stainless. Emotion rose through him in a wave of optimistic happiness. The bare hills were half hidden by a soft blue haze that made them look bigger, vaster, less earthly than they really were. He saw silver streaks in the valleys that he knew were distant streams and lakes. Birds soared between. The dazzling air seemed painted with exhilarating light and colour. The very clouds were floating gossamer that he could touch. There were bees and dragon-flies and fluttering thistle-down. Heat vibrated. His body, his physical sensations, so-called, retired into almost nothing. He felt himself, like his surroundings, made of air and sunlight. A delicious sense of resignation poured upon him. He, too, like his surroundings, was composed of air and sunshine, of insect wings, of soft, fluttering vibrations that the gorgeous spring day produced... It seemed that he renounced the heavy dues of bodily life, and enjoyed the delights, momentarily at any rate, of a more ethereal consciousness.

Near at hand, the hills were covered with the faded gold of last year's bracken, which ran down in a brimming flood till it was lost in the fresh green of the familiar woods below. Far in the hazy distance swam the sea of ash and hazel. The silver birch sprinkled that lower world with fairy light.

Yes, it was all natural enough. He could see the road quite clearly now, only a hundred yards away from where he lay. How straight it ran along the top of the hill! The landlord's expression recurred to him: "Straight as a spear." Somehow, the phrase seemed to describe exactly the Romans and all their works... The Romans, yes, and all their works...

He became aware of a sudden sympathy with these long dead conquerors of the world. With them, he felt sure, there had been no useless, foolish talk. They had known no empty words, no bandying of foolish phrases. "War to end war," and "Regeneration of the race"—no hypocritical nonsense of that sort had troubled their minds and purposes. They had not attempted to cover up the horrible in words. With them had been no childish, vain pretence. They had gone straight to their ends.

Other thoughts, too, stole over him, as he sat gazing down upon the track of that ancient road; strange thoughts, not wholly welcome. New, yet old, emotions rose in a tide upon him. He began to wonder... Had he, after all, become brutalised by the War? He knew quite well that the little "Christianity" he inherited had soon fallen from him like a garment in France. In his attitude to Life and Death he had become, frankly, pagan. He now realised, abruptly, another thing as well: in reality he had never been a "Christian" at any time. Given to him with his mother's milk, he had never accepted, felt at home with Christian dogmas. To him they had always been an alien creed. Christianity met none of his requirements..."

But what were his "requirements"? He found it difficult to answer.

Something, at any rate, different and more primitive, he thought...

Even up here, alone on the mountain-top, it was hard to be absolutely frank with himself. With a kind of savage, honest determination, he bent himself to the task. It became suddenly important for him. He must know exactly where he stood. It seemed he had reached a turning point in his life. The War, in the objective world, had been one such turning point; now he had reached another, in the subjective life, and it was more important than the first.

As he lay there in the pleasant sunshine, his thoughts went back to the fighting. A friend, he recalled, had divided people into those who enjoyed the War and those who didn't. He was obliged to admit that he had been one of the former—he had thoroughly enjoyed it. Brought up from a youth as an engineer, he had taken to a soldier's life as a duck takes to water. There had been plenty of misery, discomfort, wretchedness; but there had been compensations that, for him, outweighed them. The fierce excitement, the primitive, naked passions, the wild fury, the reckless indifference to pain and death, with the loss of the normal, cautious, pettifogging little daily self all these involved, had satisfied him. Even the actual killing...

He started. A slight shudder ran down his back as the cool wind from the open moorlands came sighing across the soft spring sunshine. Sitting up straight, he looked behind him a moment, as with an effort to turn away from something he disliked and dreaded because it was, he knew, too strong for him. But the same instant he turned round again. He faced the vile and dreadful thing in himself he had hitherto sought to deny, evade. Pretence fell away. He could not disguise from himself, that he had thoroughly enjoyed the killing; or, at any rate, had not been shocked by it as by an unnatural and ghastly duty. The shooting and bombing he performed with an effort always, but the rarer moments when he had been able to use the bayonet... the joy of feeling the steel go home...

He started again, hiding his face a moment in his hands, but he did not try to evade the hideous memories that surged. At times, he knew, he had gone quite mad with the lust of slaughter; he had gone on long after he should have stopped. Once an officer had pulled him up sharply for it, but the next instant had been killed by a bullet. He thought he had gone on killing, but he did not know. It was all a red mist before his eyes and he could only remember the sticky feeling of the blood on his hands when he gripped his rifle...

And now, at this moment of painful honesty with himself, he realised that his creed, whatever it was, must cover all that; it must provide some sort of a philosophy for it; must neither apologise nor ignore it. The heaven that it promised must be a man's heaven. The Christian heaven made no appeal to him, he could not believe in it. The ritual must be simple and direct. He felt that in some dim way he understood why those old people had thrown their captives from the Crag. The sacrifice of an animal victim that could be eaten afterwards with due ceremonial did not shock him. Such methods seemed simple, natural, effective. Yet would it not have been better—the horrid thought rose unbidden in his inmost mind—better to have cut their throats with a flint knife... slowly?

Horror-stricken, he sprang to his feet. These terrible thoughts he could not recognise as his own. Had he slept a moment in the sunlight, dreaming them? Was it some hideous nightmare flash that touched him as he dozed a second? Something of fear and awe stole over him. He stared round for some minutes into the emptiness of the desolate landscape, then hurriedly ran down to the road, hoping to exorcise the strange sudden horror by vigorous movement. Yet when he reached the track he knew that he had not succeeded. The awful pictures were gone perhaps, but the mood remained. It was as though some new attitude began to take definite form and harden within him.

He walked on, trying to pretend to himself that he was some forgotten legionary marching up with his fellows to defend the Wall. Half unconsciously he fell into the steady tramping pace of his old regiment:

the words of the ribald songs they had sung going to the front came pouring into his mind. Steadily and almost mechanically he swung along till he saw the Stone as a black speck on the left of the track, and the instant he saw it there rose in him the feeling that he stood upon the edge of an adventure that he feared yet longed for. He approached the great granite monolith with a curious thrill of anticipatory excitement, born he knew not whence.

But, of course, there was nothing. Common sense, still operating strongly, had warned him there would be, could be, nothing. In the waste the great Stone stood upright, solitary, forbidding, as it had stood for thousands of years. It dominated the landscape somewhat ominously. The sheep and cattle had used it as a rubbing-stone, and bits of hair and wool clung to its rough, weather-eaten edges; the feet of generations had worn a cup-shaped hollow at its base. The wind sighed round it plaintively. Its bulk glistened as it took the sun.

A short mile away the Blood Tarn was now plainly visible; he could see the little holm lying in a direct line with the Stone, while, overhanging the water as a dark shadow on one side, rose the cliff-like rock they called "the Crag." Of the house the landlord had mentioned, however, he could see no trace, as he relieved his shoulders of the knapsack and sat down to enjoy his lunch. The tarn, he reflected, was certainly a gloomy place; he could understand that the simple superstitious shepherds did not dare to live there, for even on this bright spring day it wore a dismal and forbidding look. With failing light, when the Crag sprawled its big lengthening shadow across the water, he could well imagine they would give it the widest possible berth. He strolled down to the shore after lunch, smoking his pipe lazily—then suddenly stood still. At the far end, hidden hitherto by a fold in the ground, he saw the little house, a faint column of blue smoke rising from the chimney, and at the same moment a woman came out of the low door and began to walk towards the tarn. She had seen him, she was moving evidently in his direction; a few minutes later she stopped and stood waiting on the path—waiting, he well knew, for him.

And his earlier mood, the mood he dreaded yet had forced himself to recognise, came back upon him with sudden redoubled power. As in some vivid dream that dominates and paralyses the will, or as in the first stages of an imposed hypnotic spell, all question, hesitation, refusal sank away. He felt a pleasurable resignation steal upon him with soft, numbing effect. Denial and criticism ceased to operate, and common sense died with them. He yielded his being automatically to the deeps of an adventure he did not understand. He began to walk towards the woman.

It was, he saw as he drew nearer, the figure of a young girl, nineteen or twenty years of age, who stood there motionless with her eyes fixed steadily on his own. She looked as wild and picturesque as the scene that framed her. Thick black hair hung loose over her back and shoulders; about her head was bound a green ribbon; her clothes consisted of a jersey and a very short skirt which showed her bare legs browned by exposure to the sun and wind. A pair of rough sandals covered her feet. Whether the face was beautiful or not he could not tell; he only knew that it attracted him immensely and with a strength of appeal that he at once felt curiously irresistible. She remained motionless against the boulder, staring fixedly at him till he was close before her. Then she spoke:

"I am glad that you have come at last," she said in a clear, strong voice that yet was soft and even tender. "We have been expecting you."

"You have been expecting me!" he repeated, astonished beyond words, yet finding the language natural, right and true. A stream of sweet feeling invaded him, his heart beat faster, he felt happy and at home in some extraordinary way he could not understand yet did not question.

"Of course," she answered, looking straight into his eyes with welcome unashamed. Her next words thrilled him to the core of his being. "I have made the room ready for you."

Quick upon her own, however, flashed back the landlord's words, while common sense made a last faint effort in his thought. He was the victim of some absurd mistake evidently. The lonely life, the forbidding surroundings, the associations of the desolate hills had affected her mind. He remembered the accident.

"I am afraid," he offered, lamely enough, "there is some mistake. I am not the friend you were expecting. I—" He stopped. A thin slight sound as of distant laughter seemed to echo behind the unconvincing words.

"There is no mistake," the girl answered firmly, with a quiet smile, moving a step nearer to him, so that he caught the subtle perfume of her vigorous youth. "I saw you clearly in the Mystery Stone. I recognised you at once."

"The Mystery Stone," he heard himself saying, bewilderment increasing, a sense of wild happiness growing with it.

Laughing, she took his hand in hers. "Come," she said, drawing him along with her, "come home with me. My father will be waiting for us; he will tell you everything, and better far than I can."

He went with her, feeling that he was made of sunlight and that he walked on air, for at her touch his own hand responded as with a sudden fierceness of pleasure that he failed utterly to understand, yet did not question for an instant. Wildly, absurdly, madly it flashed across his mind: "This is the woman I shall marry—*my* woman. I am her man."

They walked in silence for a little, for no words of any sort offered themselves to his mind, nor did the girl attempt to speak. The total absence of embarrassment between them occurred to him once or twice as curious, though the very idea of embarrassment then disappeared entirely. It all seemed natural and unforced, the sudden intercourse as familiar and effortless as though they had known one another always.

"The Mystery Stone," he heard himself saying presently, as the idea rose again to the surface of his mind. "I should like to know more about it. Tell me, dear."

"I bought it with the other things," she replied softly.

"What other things?"

She turned and looked up into his face with a slight expression of surprise; their shoulders touched as they swung along; her hair blew in the wind across his coat. "The bronze collar," she answered in the low voice that pleased him so, "and this ornament that I wear in my hair."

He glanced down to examine it. Instead of a ribbon, as he had first supposed, he saw that it was a circlet of bronze, covered with a beautiful green patina and evidently very old. In front, above the forehead, was a small disk bearing an inscription he could not decipher at the moment. He bent down and kissed her hair, the girl smiling with happy contentment, but offering no sign of resistance or annoyance.

"And," she added suddenly, "the dagger."

Holt started visibly. This time there was a thrill in her voice that seemed to pierce down straight into his heart. He said nothing, however. The unexpectedness of the word she used, together with the note in her voice that moved him so strangely, had a disconcerting effect that kept him silent for a time. He did not ask about the dagger. Something prevented his curiosity finding expression in speech, though the word, with the marked accent she placed upon it, had struck into him like the shock of sudden steel itself, causing him an indecipherable emotion of both joy and pain. He asked instead, presently, another question, and a very commonplace one: he asked where she and her father had lived before they came to these lonely hills. And the form of his question—his voice shook a little as he said it—was, again, an effort of his normal self to maintain its already precarious balance.

The effect of his simple query, the girl's reply above all, increased in him the mingled sensations of sweetness and menace, of joy and dread, that half alarmed, half satisfied him. For a moment she wore a puzzled expression, as though making an effort to remember.

"Down by the sea," she answered slowly, thoughtfully, her voice very low. "Somewhere by a big harbour with great ships coming in and out. It was there we had the break—the shock—an accident that broke us, shattering the dream we share Today." Her face cleared a little. "We were in a chariot," she went on more easily and rapidly, "and father—my father was injured, so that I went with him to a palace beyond the Wall till he grew well."

"You were in a chariot?" Holt repeated. "Surely not."

"Did I say chariot?" the girl replied. "How foolish of me!" She shook her hair back as though the gesture helped to clear her mind and memory. "That belongs, of course, to the other dream. No, not a chariot; it was a car. But it had wheels like a chariot—the old war-chariots. You know."

"Disk-wheels," thought Holt to himself. He did not ask about the palace. He asked instead where she had bought the Mystery Stone, as she called it, and the other things. Her reply bemused and enticed him farther, for he could not unravel it. His whole inner attitude was shifting with uncanny rapidity and completeness. They walked together, he now realised, with linked arms, moving slowly in step, their bodies touching. He felt the blood run hot and almost savage in his veins. He was aware how amazingly precious she was to him, how deeply, absolutely necessary to his life and happiness. Her words went past him in the mountain wind like flying birds.

"My father was fishing," she went on, "and I was on my way to join him, when the old woman called me into her dwelling and showed me the things. She wished to give them to me, but I refused the present and paid for them in gold. I put the fillet on my head to see if it would fit, and took the Mystery Stone in my hand. Then, as I looked deep into the stone, this present dream died all away. It faded out. I saw the older dreams again—*our* dreams."

"The older dreams!" interrupted Holt. "Ours!" But instead of saying the words aloud, they issued from his lips in a quiet whisper, as though control of his voice had passed a little from him. The sweetness in him became more wonderful, unmanageable; his astonishment had vanished; he walked and talked with his old familiar happy Love, the woman he had sought so long and waited for, the woman who was his mate, as he was hers, she who alone could satisfy his inmost soul.

"The old dream," she replied, "the very old—the oldest of all per- haps—when we committed the terrible sacrilege. I saw the High Priest lying dead—whom my father slew—and the other whom *you* destroyed. I saw you prise out the jewel from the image of the god—with your short bloody spear. I saw, too, our flight to the galley through the hot, awful night beneath the stars—and our escape…"

Her voice died away and she fell silent.

"Tell me more," he whispered, drawing her closer against his side. "What had *you* done?" His heart was racing now. Some fighting blood surged uppermost. He felt that he could kill, and the joy of violence and slaughter rose in him.

"Have you forgotten so completely?" she asked very low, as he pressed her more tightly still against his heart. And almost beneath her breath she whispered into his ear, which he bent to catch the little sound: "I had broken my vows with you."

"What else, my lovely one—my best beloved—what more did you see?" he whispered in return, yet wondering why the fierce pain and anger that he felt behind still lay hidden from betrayal.

"Dream after dream, and always we were punished. But the last time was the clearest, for it was here—here where we now walk together in the sunlight and the wind—it was here the savages hurled us from the rock."

A shiver ran through him, making him tremble with an unaccountable touch of cold that communicated itself to her as well. Her arm went instantly about his shoulder, as he stooped and kissed her passionately. "Fasten your coat about you," she said tenderly, but with troubled breath, when he released her, "for this wind is chill although the sun shines brightly. We were glad, you remember, when they stopped to kill us, for we were tired and our feet were cut to pieces by the long, rough journey from the Wall." Then suddenly her voice grew louder again and the smile of happy confidence came back into her eyes. There was the deep earnestness of love in it, of love that cannot end or die. She looked up into his face. "But soon now," she said, "we shall be free. For you have come, and it is nearly finished—this weary little present dream."

"How," he asked, "shall we get free?" A red mist swam momentarily before his eyes.

"My father," she replied at once, "will tell you all. It is quite easy."

"Your father, too, remembers?"

"The moment the collar touches him," she said, "he is a priest again. See! Here he comes forth already to meet us, and to bid you welcome."

Holt looked up, startled. He had hardly noticed, so absorbed had he been in the words that half intoxicated him, the distance they had covered. The cottage was now close at hand, and a tall, powerfully built man, wearing a shepherd's rough clothing, stood a few feet in front of him. His stature, breadth of shoulder and thick black beard made up a striking figure. The dark eyes, with fire in them, gazed straight into his own, and a kindly smile played round the stern and vigorous mouth.

"Greeting, my son," said a deep, booming voice, "for I shall call you my son as I did of old. The bond of the spirit is stronger than that of the flesh, and with us three the tie is indeed of triple strength. You come, too, at an auspicious hour, for the omens are favourable and the time of our liberation is at hand." He took the other's hand in a grip that might have killed an ox and yet was warm with gentle kindliness, while Holt, now caught wholly into the spirit of some deep reality he could not master yet accepted, saw that the wrist was small, the fingers shapely, the gesture itself one of dignity and refinement.

"Greeting, my father," he replied, as naturally as though he said more modern words.

"Come in with me, I pray," pursued the other, leading the way, "and let me show you the poor accommodation we have provided, yet the best that we can offer."

He stooped to pass the threshold, and as Holt stooped likewise the girl took his hand and he knew that his bewitchment was complete. Entering the low doorway, he passed through a kitchen, where only the roughest, scantiest furniture was visible, into another room that was completely bare. A heap of dried bracken had been spread on the floor in one corner to form a bed. Beside it lay two cheap, coloured blankets. There was nothing else.

"Our place is poor," said the man, smiling courteously, but with that dignity and air of welcome which made the hovel seem a palace. "Yet it may serve, perhaps, for the short time that you will need it. Our little dream here is well-nigh over, now that you have come. The long weary pilgrimage at last draws to a close." The girl had left them alone a moment, and the man stepped closer to his guest. His face grew solemn, his voice deeper and more earnest suddenly, the light in his eyes seemed actually to flame with the enthusiasm of a great belief. "Why have you tarried thus so long, and where?" he asked in a lowered tone that vibrated in the little space. "We have sought you with prayer and fasting, and she has spent her nights for you in tears. You lost the way, it must be. The lesser dreams entangled your feet, I see." A touch of sadness entered the voice, the eyes held pity in them. "It is, alas, too easy, I well know," he murmured. "It is too easy."

"I lost the way," the other replied. It seemed suddenly that his heart was filled with fire. "But now," he cried aloud, "now that I have found her, I will never, never let her go again. My feet are steady and my way is sure."

"For ever and ever, my son," boomed the happy, yet almost solemn answer, "she is yours. Our freedom is at hand."

He turned and crossed the little kitchen again, making a sign that his guest should follow him. They stood together by the door, looking out across the tarn in silence. The afternoon sunshine fell in a golden blaze across the bare hills that seemed to smoke with the glory of the fiery light. But the Crag loomed dark in shadow overhead, and the little lake lay deep and black beneath it.

"Acella, Acella!" called the man, the name breaking upon his companion as with a shock of sweet delicious fire that filled his entire being, as the girl came the same instant from behind the cottage. "The Gods call me," said her father. "I go now to the hill. Protect our guest and comfort him in my absence."

Without another word, he strode away up the hillside and presently was visible standing on the summit of the Crag, his arms stretched out above his head to heaven, his great head thrown back, his bearded face turned upwards. An impressive, even a majestic figure he looked, as his bulk and stature rose in dark silhouette against the brilliant evening sky. Holt stood motionless, watching him for several minutes, his heart swelling in his breast, his pulses thumping before some great nameless pressure that rose from the depths of his being. That inner attitude which seemed a new and yet more satisfying attitude to life than he had known hitherto, had crystallised. Define it he could not, he only knew that he accepted it as natural. It satisfied him. The sight of that dignified, gaunt figure worshipping upon the hill-top enflamed him...

"I have brought the stone," a voice interrupted his reflections, and turning, he saw the girl beside him. She held out for his inspection a dark square object that looked to him at first like a black stone lying against the brown skin of her hand. "The Mystery Stone," the girl added, as their faces bent down together to examine it. "It is there I see the dreams I told you of."

He took it from her and found that it was heavy, composed apparently of something like black quartz, with a brilliant polished surface that revealed clear depths within. Once, evidently, it had been set in a stand or frame, for the marks where it had been attached still showed, and it was obviously of great age. He felt confused, the mind in him troubled yet excited, as he gazed. The effect upon him was as though a wind rose suddenly and passed across his inmost subjective life, setting its entire contents in rushing motion.

"And here," the girl said, "is the dagger."

He took from her the short bronze weapon, feeling at once instinctively its ragged edge, its keen point, sharp and effective still. The handle had long since rotted away, but the bronze tongue, and the holes where the rivets had been, remained, and, as he touched it, the confusion and trouble in his mind increased to a kind of turmoil, in which violence, linked to something tameless, wild and almost savage, was the dominating emotion. He turned to seize the girl and crush her to him in a passionate embrace, but she held away, throwing back her lovely head, her eyes shining, her lips parted, yet one hand stretched out to stop him.

"First look into it with me," she said quietly. "Let us see together."

She sat down on the turf beside the cottage door, and Holt, obeying, took his place beside her. She remained very still for some minutes, covering the stone with both hands as though to warm it. Her lips moved. She seemed to be repeating some kind of invocation beneath her breath, though no actual words were audible. Presently her hands parted. They sat together gazing at the polished surface. They looked within.

"There comes a white mist in the heart of the stone," the girl whispered. "It will soon open. The pictures will then grow. Look!" she exclaimed after a brief pause, "they are forming now."

"I see only mist," her companion murmured, gazing intently. "Only mist I see."

She took his hand and instantly the mist parted. He found himself peering into another landscape which opened before his eyes as though it were a photograph. Hills covered with heather stretched away on every side.

"Hills, I see," he whispered. "The ancient hills—"

"Watch closely," she replied, holding his hand firmly.

At first the landscape was devoid of any sign of life; then suddenly it surged and swarmed with moving figures. Torrents of men poured over the hill-crests and down their heathery sides in columns. He could see them clearly—great hairy men, clad in skins, with thick shields on their left arms or slung over their backs, and short stabbing spears in their hands. Thousands upon thousands poured over in an endless stream. In the distance he could see other columns sweeping in a turning movement. A few of the men rode rough ponies and seemed to be directing the march, and these, he knew, were the chiefs...

The scene grew dimmer, faded, died away completely. Another took its place:

By the faint light he knew that it was dawn. The undulating country, less hilly than before, was still wild and uncultivated. A great wall, with towers at intervals, stretched away till it was lost in shadowy distance. On the nearest of these towers he saw a sentinel clad in armour, gazing out across the rolling country. The armour gleamed faintly in the pale glimmering light, as the man suddenly snatched up a bugle and blew upon it. From a brazier burning beside him he next seized a brand and fired a great heap of brushwood. The smoke rose in a dense column into the air almost immediately, and from all directions, with incredible rapidity, figures came pouring up to man the wall. Hurriedly they strung their bows, and laid spare arrows close beside them on the coping. The light grew brighter. The whole country was alive with savages; like the waves of the sea they came rolling in enormous numbers. For several minutes the wall held. Then, in an impetuous, fearful torrent, they poured over...

It faded, died away, was gone again, and a moment later yet another took its place:

But this time the landscape was familiar, and he recognised the tarn. He saw the savages upon the ledge that flanked the dominating Crag; they had three captives with them. He saw two men. The other was a woman. But the woman had fallen exhausted to the ground, and a chief on a rough pony rode back to see what had delayed the march. Glancing at the captives, he made a fierce gesture with his arm towards the water far below. Instantly the woman was jerked cruelly to her feet and forced onwards till the summit of the Crag was reached. A man snatched something from her hand. A second later she was hurled over the brink.

The two men were next dragged on to the dizzy spot where she had stood. Dead with fatigue, bleeding from numerous wounds, yet at this awful moment they straightened themselves, casting contemptuous glances at the fierce savages surrounding them. They were Romans and would die like Romans. Holt saw their faces clearly for the first time.

He sprang up with a cry of anguished fury.

"The second man!" he exclaimed. "You saw the second man!"

The girl, releasing his hand, turned her eyes slowly up to his, so that he met the flame of her ancient and undying love shining like stars upon him out of the night of time.

"Ever since that moment," she said in a low voice that trembled, "I have been looking, waiting for you—"

He took her in his arms and smothered her words with kisses, holding her fiercely to him as though he would never let her go. "I, too," he said, his whole being burning with his love, "I have been looking, waiting for you. Now I have found you. We have found each other...!"

The dusk fell slowly, imperceptibly. As twilight slowly draped the gaunt hills, blotting out familiar details, so the strong dream, veil upon veil, drew closer over the soul of the wanderer, obliterating finally the last reminder of Today. The little wind had dropped and the desolate moors lay silent, but for the hum of distant water falling to its valley bed. His life, too, and the life of the girl, he knew, were similarly falling, falling into some deep shadowed bed where rest would come at last. No details troubled him, he asked himself no questions. A profound sense of happy peace numbed every nerve and stilled his beating heart.

He felt no fear, no anxiety, no hint of alarm or uneasiness vexed his singular contentment. He realised one thing only—that the girl lay in his arms, he held her fast, her breath mingled with his own. They had found each other. What else mattered?

From time to time, as the daylight faded and the sun went down behind the moors, she spoke. She uttered words he vaguely heard, listening, though with a certain curious effort, before he closed the thing she said with kisses. Even the fierceness of his blood was gone. The world lay still, life almost ceased to flow. Lapped in the deeps of his great love, he was redeemed, perhaps, of violence and savagery...

"Three dark birds," she whispered, "pass across the sky... they fall beyond the ridge. The omens are favourable. A hawk now follows them, cleaving the sky with pointed wings."

"A hawk," he murmured. "The badge of my old Legion."

"My father will perform the sacrifice," he heard again, though it seemed a long interval had passed, and the man's figure was now invisible on the Crag amid the gathering darkness. "Already he prepares the fire. Look, the sacred island is alight. He has the black cock ready for the knife."

Holt roused himself with difficulty, lifting his face from the garden of her hair. A faint light, he saw, gleamed fitfully on the holm within the tarn. Her father, then, had descended from the Crag, and had lit the sacrificial fire upon the stones. But what did the doings of the father matter now to him?

"The dark bird," he repeated dully, "the black victim the Gods of the Underworld alone accept. It is good, Acella, it is good!" He was about to sink back again, taking her against his breast as before, when she resisted and sat up suddenly.

"It is time," she said aloud. "The hour has come. My father climbs, and we must join him on the summit. Come!"

She took his hand and raised him to his feet, and together they began the rough ascent towards the Crag. As they passed along the shore of the Tarn of Blood, he saw the fire reflected in the ink-black waters; he made out, too, though dimly, a rough circle of big stones, with a larger flag-stone lying in the centre. Three small fires of bracken and wood, placed in a triangle with its apex towards the Standing Stone on the distant hill, burned briskly, the crackling material sending out sparks that pierced the columns of thick smoke. And in this smoke, peering, shifting, appearing and disappearing, it seemed he saw great faces moving. The flickering light and twirling smoke made clear sight difficult. His bliss, his lethargy were very deep. They left the tarn below them and hand in hand began to climb the final slope.

Whether the physical effort of climbing disturbed the deep pressure of the mood that numbed his senses, or whether the cold draught of wind they met upon the ridge restored some vital detail of Today, Holt does not know. Something, at any rate, in him wavered suddenly, as though a centre of gravity had shifted slightly. There was a perceptible alteration in the balance of thought and feeling that had held invariable now for many hours. It seemed to him that something heavy lifted, or rather, began to lift—a weight, a shadow, something oppressive that obstructed light. A ray of light, as it were, struggled through the thick darkness that enveloped him. To him, as he paused on the ridge to recover his breath, came this vague suggestion of faint light breaking across the blackness. It was objective.

"See," said the girl in a low voice, "the moon is rising. It lights the sacred island. The blood-red waters turn to silver."

He saw, indeed, that a huge three-quarter moon now drove with almost visible movement above the distant line of hills; the little tarn gleamed as with silvery armour; the glow of the sacrificial fires showed red across it. He looked down with a shudder into the sheer depth that opened at his feet, then turned to look at his companion. He started and shrank back. Her face, lit by the moon and by the fire, shone pale as death; her black hair framed it with a terrible suggestiveness; the eyes, though brilliant as ever, had a film upon them. She stood in an attitude of both ecstasy and resignation, and one outstretched arm pointed towards the summit where her father stood.

Her lips parted, a marvellous smile broke over her features, her voice was suddenly unfamiliar: "He wears the collar," she uttered. "Come. Our time is here at last, and we are ready. See, he waits for us!"

There rose for the first time struggle and opposition in him; he resisted the pressure of her hand that had seized his own and drew him forcibly along. Whence came the resistance and the opposition he could not tell, but though he followed her, he was aware that the refusal in him strengthened. The weight of darkness that oppressed him shifted a little more, an inner light increased. The same moment they reached the summit and stood beside—the priest. There was a curious sound of fluttering. The figure, he saw, was naked, save for a rough blanket tied loosely about the waist.

"The hour has come at last," cried his deep booming voice that woke echoes from the dark hills about them. "We are alone now with our Gods." And he broke then into a monotonous rhythmic chanting that rose and fell upon the wind, yet in a tongue that sounded strange; his erect figure swayed slightly with its cadences; his black beard swept his naked chest; and his face, turned skywards, shone in the mingled light of moon above and fire below, yet with an added light as well that burned within him rather than without. He was a weird, magnificent figure, a priest of ancient rites invoking his deathless deities upon the unchanging hills.

But upon Holt, too, as he stared in awed amazement, an inner light had broken suddenly. It came as with a dazzling blaze that at first paralysed thought and action. His mind cleared, but too abruptly for movement, either of tongue or hand, to be possible. Then, abruptly, the inner darkness rolled away completely. The light in the wild eyes of the great chanting, swaying figure, he now knew was the light of mania.

The faint fluttering sound increased, and the voice of the girl was oddly mingled with it. The priest had ceased his invocation. Holt, aware that he stood alone, saw the girl go past him carrying a big black bird that struggled with vainly beating wings.

"Behold the sacrifice," she said, as she knelt before her father and held up the victim. "May the Gods accept it as presently They shall accept us too!"

The great figure stooped and took the offering, and with one blow of the knife he held, its head was severed from its body. The blood spattered on the white face of the kneeling girl. Holt was aware for the first time that she, too, was now unclothed; but for a loose blanket, her white body gleamed against the dark heather in the moonlight. At the same moment she rose to her feet, stood upright, turned towards him so that he saw the dark hair streaming across her naked shoulders, and, with a face of ecstasy, yet ever that strange film upon her eyes, her voice came to him on the wind:

"Farewell, yet not farewell! We shall meet, all three, in the underworld. The Gods accept us!"

Turning her face away, she stepped towards the ominous figure behind, and bared her ivory neck and breast to the knife. The eyes of the maniac were upon her own; she was as helpless and obedient as a lamb before his spell.

Then Holt's horrible paralysis, if only just in time, was lifted. The priest had raised his arm, the bronze knife with its ragged edge gleamed in the air, with the other hand he had already gathered up the thick dark hair, so that the neck lay bare and open to the final blow. But it was two other details, Holt thinks, that set his muscles suddenly free, enabling him to act with the swift judgment which, being wholly unexpected, disconcerted both maniac and victim and frustrated the awful culmination. The dark spots of blood upon the face he loved, and the sudden final fluttering of the dead bird's wings upon the ground—these two things, life actually touching death, released the held-back springs.

He leaped forward. He received the blow upon his left arm and hand. It was his right fist that sent the High Priest to earth with a blow that, luckily, felled him in the direction away from the dreadful brink, and it was his right arm and hand, he became aware some time afterwards only, that were chiefly of use in carrying the fainting girl and her unconscious father back to the shelter of the cottage, and to the best help and comfort he could provide...

It was several years afterwards, in a very different setting, that he found himself spelling out slowly to a little boy the lettering cut into a circlet of bronze the child found on his study table. To the child he told a fairy tale, then dismissed him to play with his mother in the garden. But, when alone, he rubbed away the verdigris with great care, for the circlet was thin and frail with age, as he examined again the little picture of a tripod from which smoke issued, incised neatly in the metal. Below it, almost as sharp as when the Roman craftsman cut it first, was the name Acella. He touched the letters tenderly with his left hand, from which two fingers were missing, then placed it in a drawer of his desk and turned the key.

"That curious name," said a low voice behind his chair. His wife had come in and was looking over his shoulder. "You love it, and I dread it." She sat on the desk beside him, her eyes troubled. "It was the name father used to called me in his illness."

Her husband looked at her with passionate tenderness, but said no word.

"And this," she went on, taking the broken hand in both her own, "is the price you paid to me for his life. I often wonder what strange good deity brought you upon the lonely moor that night, and just in the very nick of time. You remember...?"

"The deity who helps true lovers, of course," he said with a smile, evading the question. The deeper memory, he knew, had closed absolutely in her since the moment of the attempted double crime. He kissed her, murmuring to himself as he did so, but too low for her to hear, "Acella! *My* Acella...!"

# THE SHADOW ON THE MOOR

## Stuart Strauss

There is very little information available about Strauss. Even E. F. Bleiler's comprehensive volume *Science Fiction: The Early Years* (1990) simply says "No information" in regard to him. Strauss, which was presumably a pseudonym, is known to us solely through his three publications in *Weird Tales*, two in 1928 and one in 1934. "The Clenched Hand" (1928) is a supernatural murder mystery, while "The Soul Tube" (1934) is an occult science fiction tale. "The Shadow on the Moor" was published in the February 1928 edition of *Weird Tales*, who described it as "A creepy tale of the pre-Druidic ruins of England—out on the moor were dancing, and strange wild music, and death."

The stillness of the room was broken only by the clicking of a typewriter, which went on uninterruptedly for some time. Finally a man arose, and, stretching himself, yawned and spoke to his companion.

"It's too hot to work tonight, and, besides, who could write a horror story on a night like this?"

The other man raised his eyes from his book.

"I suppose it should be thundering, lightening, and raining torrents, with a wind that whistles around the housetops. Come on, let's hit the hay, Jerry."

When he had finished his preparations for bed, Jerry Jarvais slipped out upon the balcony of the inn for a final cigaret. He stood there silent, gazing off across the moor. The night was very still, and the moon flooded everything with a soft, silvery light that brought all out in a marble whiteness—a softness that hid the grime and dirt, and gave the commonplace an air of beauty unseen by the glare of day. There was only the faintest hint of a breeze that, soft as midnight velvet, whipped his dressing-gown around his legs and made the trees bend ever so gracefully, ever so slightly, seeming to bow and quiver like dancers on a polished ballroom floor.

Jarvais was silent, rapt, alone and lost in the beauty of the night. For a long time he had heard of this section of desolate country with its memories and mementos of a lost race. No other part of England held its savage charm. Jarvais had come here seeking new material, new colour, and new ideas. He had been stagnating. Before, to him, mystery had meant the East—the Orient—but here at home in the quiet of old England was more mystery—more allure than he had ever known.

Far away across the moonlit bleakness of the moor were the ruins—that mass of toppled columns and rough-hewn slabs set in crude circles. The stones glistened mistily, and threw huge, sprawling shadows beneath them like pools of blood on a silver tray.

Broken only by the whispering of the trees, the stillness gripped Jarvais; held him tense, expectant, waiting. But for what? For there was only stillness and the soft rustle of the night wind among the trees.

As Jarvais was about to toss his finished cigaret over the balcony rail and return to his room, he paused and glanced sharply across the empty lawn. He had seen something—he did not know what. There was movement, where but a moment before had been naught but moonlit emptiness. He had heard nothing, but he was conscious of another presence. He looked out again across the moor. All was as before, but here beneath the balcony was something, someone. He had caught but the fleeting glimpse of a shadow moving, where before had been but nothingness.

It was a shadow—the dim silhouette of a woman. The time was long past midnight, and the inhabitants of the inn were all asleep. What was a woman doing here, alone, on the moor at this hour? The sight of something alive, here in this deserted place, and at this hour, made him shiver. It was so out of all keeping with his thoughts and the place. Icy fingers of dread clutched his heart. Then he shrugged his shoulders and smiled. It was nothing. Some tourist out to see the moor. But what was a woman doing here alone, at this hour? None the less, here she was, moving slowly across the silvery waste toward the ruins that were so white and still in the glow of the dying moon.

Jarvais rubbed his eyes, shook his head, and looked again. The shadow was still there, but becoming fainter, and more distant. He paused, and suddenly a thought came to him. Shadows were cast by bodies; they were mere reflections of a concrete shape. Perhaps a wind-blown tree had cast it. But the shadow, which seemed a woman, was bodiless. There was only the shadow, and no figure. There were now no trees near the shadow to cast such strange reflections. To find that the shadow was actually bodiless brought back all his first terror—the sense of dread that he had first experienced. This was not earthly. It was uncanny. Impossible. Yet his eyes told him that the impossible was fact.

Through his mind raced all the tales he had heard of this lonely, lovely country, of things that should be dead, but lived; things spoken of only in whispers, and never to be mentioned. The shadow was moving toward the ruins. What was happening here beneath his window—strange, weird, terrorising? There was but one thing to do—follow.

Silently he dropped over the rail of the low balcony, caught up with and followed behind the shadow of the woman, if woman it were.

It seemed to Jarvais that this ghostly pursuit lasted for hours. Now he would lose it and would wait. Then in a few moments he would see the dim outlines again before him, always moving toward that heap of rocks—the ruins that had held his fancy with their starkness. Now and then clouds scudded across the face of the moon, and the moor took on strange lights and patches of colour.

On and on he followed, and suddenly stopped dead-still, for in the place of the one shadow there now were many, all hurrying in the same direction toward the ruins—bodiless shapes that moved noiselessly before him.

Now that they were nearing the ruins, Jarvais could make out how crude they were, how rough-hewn; yet withal they held a subtle sense of majestic power, of latent evil; a sense of darkness and decay; a sense of age and forgotten secrets. He wondered who were the people that had built them, what strange gods they had worshipped here, and how many savage cries of exultation had risen on the still, moonlit air, and echoed far across the now deserted moor.

From out of the stillness came a weird sound—then music soft and low in the distance, soft and yet with an eery strain that chilled his blood and echoed in his brain. The music increased its beat and time, and in it were savagery and cries of lust and forbidden desires. The shadows, with Jarvais close behind, were approaching the ruins, coming closer, ever closer, and the moon now setting in the west cast pale rays on the rude stones that lay sprawling in drunken rings. The music became more terrible, tore at his brain like iron fingers. Strange voices whispered of uncanny, revolting mysteries; obscene shapes floated before his eyes. Ever, ever the music hammered at his brain. He stumbled and nearly fell. The gibbering in his ears increased, became more awful, more degrading, more passionately revolting. The music throbbed through all his senses. Frenzy swayed him, and swept away his last touch of wisdom. He was a primate—one of the first men—uncivilised, terror-stricken—back in the dawn of time—back with black terror and the rolling drums.

He gave way to the madness of the music, cast aside his garments and ran as naked as the first man after the shadows that were converging in a dark mass toward the narrow entryway between two huge, rough-hewn pillars. With a cry of exultation, Jarvais sprang after them, and then it seemed to him that the whole world was shaken by a thunderclap; a heavy weight struck across his shoulder; he moved forward, stumbled, and fell. As through a mist he saw flickering lights and heard hoots and bellows, and in his brain echoed screeches and cat-calls. The music roared into a terrifying crescendo, then blackness and oblivion came upon him.

He awoke to painful consciousness, in the grey of an early dawn, shivering and cold, surprized to find himself here alone, naked upon the grey and barren moor. How had he gotten here? Then memory came back to him. He recalled how he had run screaming, naked in the moonlight; remembered the shadow, and the horror at the ruins. He looked up and saw he was lying not more than five feet from the entrance.

Seen in the light of dawn, the piles were still sinister, but not horrible—a mass of grey, tumble-down rocks and crude broken columns—sinister, but surely no terror could lurk within them. Soon Jarvais located his cast-off clothing, and wearily started to return to the inn, which he could see in the distance, but surely not the distance he had come on the preceding night. Shakily he laughed, for he must have been running around in circles. He decided he would tell no one of his nocturnal adventures.

Unobserved he gained his room, and after bathing and dressing he joined his friend for breakfast. Nothing was said concerning his experiences, and in the afternoon they returned to London.

Once more at home, Jarvais plunged into work with a new vigour, striving in it to erase from his mind the events of that night upon the moor—the night with all its unexplained, mysterious happenings and horrors, over which brooded those aged, ageless ruins. Slowly, as time passed, the thing began to slip from his memory, to be recalled only on moonlit nights, when he had stayed too long over his books.

As he was reading the paper one morning, he ran across an item that at once attracted his attention, and caused him to remember too vividly things he wished to forget, things that had tugged at his mind despite his desire to let them slip into the place of unwanted memories. The item was dated at the little village where he had spent that never-to-be-forgotten time:

### DEAD MAN FOUND ON MOOR

Early this morning the body of Charles Gilbert, living at the Blue Boar Tavern, was found on the moor near the ruined temple, naked, and his head crushed by a mammoth rock, apparently fallen from the ruins. How such a huge slab had been dislodged is one of the mysteries that surround this case. Near the body were found the nightclothes of the dead man. No motive for the crime was apparent. The mere fact of the body's being there has only deepened the mystery. Gilbert was a famous student of pre-druidistic culture and remains.

To Jarvais came an overwhelming desire to revisit the moor, to see again its sinister ruins and the bodiless shadows. He wished to solve, if possible, the enigma hidden behind those rings of crouching stones. Here was something deadly, something dangerous that had taken human life and would beyond all doubt be unappeased until more had fallen under its malevolent spell.

Quickly he packed, as if fearing he might change his mind, and returned to the little inn that nestled on the border of the sombre moor, where such strange events had taken place.

He found the place almost deserted. The mysterious death of Gilbert had frightened away the casual tourists. The innkeeper was pathetically glad to see Jarvais. He bustled up, and after having arranged with him about his room, he asked, "And what are you doing here, Mr Jarvais?"

"I came up for a rest and a little quiet, Johnson."

"Well, you'll get it here, sir. No one comes here any more after Mr Gilbert's death, sir. It's the moor. She frightens them. She's bad—is the moor. No one knows her secrets, and if they do learn—well, they don't come back, sir."

Jarvais looked at him for a moment, and then broke the silence that followed the innkeeper's last remark. "What do you know about those ruins?"

"Well, Mr Jarvais, not much, sir. But I know this: I wouldn't go there for a million pounds, I wouldn't. There's things there, sir, that a man better not talk about. There's death there and worse."

"Pshaw! Don't be an ass, Johnson," said Jarvais crossly, and climbed the stairs to his room.

After his dinner, Jarvais strolled toward the village, which lay at no great distance from the inn. Lights glimmered yellowly through shuttered windows. At every house the door was strongly barred. As the dusk deepened into darkness the few people who were upon the streets disappeared, and except for the glow of a few poor street-lamps, the village was dead and deserted.

Jarvais returned to his lodging, ready to take up his nocturnal vigil. He sat in the unlighted room, trying to pierce the mystery that lay out there on the silent moor. Downstairs the inn clock struck 2, the fire that had played so merrily upon his hearth was sending out its last dying rays, and the lights flickering over the walls made ghostlike figures that danced and rolled like souls in torture. Jarvais arose with a sigh, and opening his casement windows he stepped out upon the balcony.

The air was cold, with a touch of winter in its fingertips, but the moor was bright—brighter even than on that other night six months before. Shivering slightly, he stood waiting, with his eyes intent upon the patch of lawn where first he had seen the shadow which had no body.

Very slowly time passed. Twice he had heard the clock below stairs strike the hour. Finally Jarvais felt certain that nothing would occur this night, went to bed, and at once fell asleep.

Dream after dream pursued each other through his brain, each more horrible than the last. Queer bloated things danced with witches, and a monstrous hairy being without eyes performed strange rites. The eery music of the moor echoed in his brain, and in all these dreams the ruins had their grim and terrifying part, silently, broodingly overlooking the obscenity within the circle of crumbling rocks. He awoke in a cold sweat of terror, and lay for some time almost fearing to return to sleep, but finally he dropped off into untroubled rest.

After a meagre breakfast he mapped out his procedure for the day. He had a letter to write, and then the rest of the day to inspect the ruins. So after posting a letter to a firm in London he shouldered his knapsack of lunch and went to spend the day upon the moor.

When he reached the ruins he stood and inspected them carefully. On that sunshiny morning the grey pile of rock looked very peaceful; vines and mosses grew here and there over them; on some of the stones were crude, carven figures, and designs half obliterated by storm and decay. As he was walking around the circle of broken rocks he soon saw the gateway through which he had plunged on that never-to-be-forgotten night. He entered and found himself in a hollowed circle which was several inches below the level of the moor. Nothing was visible except hard-packed earth. Carefully he searched for footprints, but found none. Then from the inside he examined diligently each post and stone for some sign of recent use, but again he drew a blank.

Giving up his quest for the time, he ate his lunch and then continued the search as fruitlessly as before. As far as appearances showed, there had been no one here for ages. But here a thought struck him. Before the death of Gilbert the ruins had been frequently visited by tourists, and yet there was no sign of them. Certainly this was queer. It was a puzzle he could not solve.

Tiring of his useless search, he left the ruins and started for the village and the inn. As he reached the entrance of the ruins, and stooped over to pick up his knapsack, he noticed, hidden in a crevice between the stones, a fragment of paper. He picked it up and looked at it closely. It was dirty, torn and weatherbeaten, a leaf evidently torn from a notebook, for the paper was small and could very easily have fitted into the pocket. It had been carelessly torn, for only a part of a sentence was visible. The handwriting was neat and painstaking. This scrap of writing had neither beginning nor end:

"... discovered secret today; will return for further investigation tonight; the altar is—"

Then came the tear running clear across the page. In the still remaining upper corner were the initials C. G.

Evidently the dead man on the moor had found something that had eluded Jarvais. The mention of the altar puzzled him. Surely the matter was becoming more involved—more mystifying. Jarvais was as much lost in darkness as he had been before. The thing had a deeper look. He could see no beginning and no end. Placing the scrap of paper in his wallet, and turning the jumble of thoughts over in his mind, he returned to his lodgings.

*

As he opened the door, Jarvais was impressed by the bright hospitality of the place. The inn's room was cheerily alight, a huge fire blazed and flickered on the hearth, and around it, seated in a semicircle, were some of the village worthies. The smoke of their pipes wreathed about their heads.

"It is," said Jarvais to himself, "like a page straight out of Dickens."

The opening of the door caused them to turn and stare at him, and in the memorable manner of all villagers, they spoke to him courteously. Little Johnson, the innkeeper, bustled up and made a place for him around the circle, and when Jarvais had been made comfortable with a cigar and a glass of steaming toddy, the innkeeper introduced him.

"This is Mr Jarvais, the writing gentleman who wants to know somew'at o' the moor. Mr Jarvais, these are the mayor and the select-men of the village."

There was a silence for some time as though all were plunged deeply into thought. Finally an old greybeard, the mayor, shook his head and spoke.

"There ain't none of us here that knows much about her, sir, nothing at all. Except George here, and George he can't speak, poor fellow, 'cause he's dumb."

Jarvais followed the pointing finger and saw, huddled in a corner, as close to the fire as possible, a wisp of a man, so emaciated and dried up that he looked like a mummy. Countless centuries seemed to have passed over his head; how old he was Jarvais could not judge. The countenance was terrifying—not a face at all, but a ghastly caricature of a human face. Always, Jarvais thought, it would haunt his dreams. Dreadful, worse than bestial, it leered at him from across the room. The mouth, a flabby gash, from which saliva trickled down the chin, moved constantly, emitting little clucking noises. The eyes fascinated

Jarvais like the eyes of a snake; they were round, full, nearly opaque, of a dull grey glassiness shot with fine red lines.

"Why, he is blind, as well as dumb!" exclaimed Jarvais.

"That he is, sir. He walked too late on the moor one moonlight night and saw the shadows."

The last word scattered all of Jarvais' fast-disappearing equanimity. So the shadows were common gossip.

"The shadows!" he exclaimed.

"Yes, sir. They haunt the moor near the ruins and mean death or worse to such as see them."

"But, George isn't dead!"

"No, sir. He ran away before he heard the music, and don't you think he would be better dead? There be strange things on the moor, cries and shouts and lights where there ain't nothin', nor nobody. I tell you, sir, we stay clear o' the moor on the moonlight nights, sir, in the summer and late fall. Rest o' the time nothin' happens. It's best not to go out o' doors on them nights. Them ruins is terrible, they be haunted places and it be wise not to go anywhere close to them, sir. I warned Mr Gilbert, him that was killed, you know, but he wouldn't pay no attention to me and they got him."

"Who are *they*?" asked Jarvais, sensing that he was getting to the crux of the matter at last.

"They be shadows, sir; shadows that ain't got no bodies, so I hear. *I* ain't seen them yet, praise God."

Shortly after this, Jarvais, tiring of the now commonplace conversation, excused himself, and leaving the circle around the fire, went to his room. Switching on the light he noticed a package lying on his table; it was the book he had ordered from London, entitled *Pre-Druidistic Ruins in England*. Seating himself in a chair beside the shaded reading-light, he was soon deeply engrossed in his purchase. As he read on and on, he stopped with a jerk, and then re-read more carefully the following two paragraphs:

"Perhaps the most interesting of these ancient ruins are those at Humbledon, which are the earliest known, so far as we have been able to trace. How far back beyond the druids and their religion these ruins of another race and age go, we can only estimate. It is, in fact, almost impossible to tell. There is another factor that makes the piles at Humbledon of exceeding interest to students. While it is, as we have stated before, the oldest of the ruins, it is, strangely, the best preserved, and so far as investigation can go, there is no sound reason for this being the case. The carving in most cases is remarkably clear, and the dancing-ring almost in its original state.

"Here, however, we encounter the most peculiar factor in these remains. While the dancing-ring is very wonderfully preserved, the moon altar, which is the distinguishing feature of most pre-druidistic piles, is missing. The moon altar in all similar ruins discovered is a huge stone carved in the shape of a new moon. From all evidence we can gather, the victim, or the sacrifice, to term it more fitly, was tied between the horns of these altars, and then sacrificed by the sacred knife that is shown in many carvings. It, seemingly, carried a huge, crescent-shaped blade and must, from the pictures, have had an edge like a razor. In most cases the altar is found in the exact centre of the dancing-ring. There has been intensive search made for the one at Humbledon, but so far without satisfaction. The absence of the altar in this, the best preserved of all pre-druidistic remains, makes one of the most fascinating studies for the student of these things."

As he finished reading, Jarvais remembered the slip of paper he had found on the moor early that morning—that torn scrap that ended so suddenly: "the altar is—." What could the rest of the sentence be? What was lost by his not having the remaining fragment? Undoubtedly Gilbert had found the answer to the puzzle and the answer to the great secret of the moor—the secret that had eluded all the other students and archaeologists. Why, here in the best preserved of all these ruins, was there no moon altar? Even in the most ravaged of the others, the altar was conspicuous, but here none could be found.

At last Jarvais arose and stretched himself. He was cramped and tired. He looked at his watch. It was after 2. He had sat engrossed in his reading longer than he had realised.

Pulling on a sweater, Jarvais opened his casements and stepped upon the balcony. Again it was moonlight, for this was the season of the moon, when bright nights were common and the people of the village kept behind barred doors. The moor was white, cold, and apparently tenantless. The night was very still. Not even the breath of a breeze stirred the trees, and the shadows of the buildings and the shrubbery were solid black patches of darkness on the silver lawn. Over the moor, far in the distance, were the ruins, clear-cut and white beneath the moon. But there was always about them, Jarvais thought, a majestic power holding threats, and a menace of dark deeds still unfulfilled.

He stood looking intently at the patch of lawn where first he had seen the shadow. He waited for what seemed to him hours; then, as his glance wandered and came back, he saw it! The shadow!

Again it was a woman who moved apparently stealthily across the lawn, but over the moor, ever toward the ruins. Stealthily Jarvais followed after her. Emulating Ulysses, he had stuffed his ears with cotton, because he had no desire to hear the throb of the music that turned his blood to flame. On and on he followed the ghostly chase. As before, he pursued the shadow, now losing it in some patch of darkness, now seeing it once more as it crossed an open place—on and on, keeping well behind the bodiless woman. Though he could not hear, he could sense that now the music was swelling out over the moor. Because of the cotton in his ears, he remained unmoved. The pace of the shadow quickened and he hastened after it.

They were now at the gateway. For some time Jarvais had been noticing the growing number of shadowy forms. The space before the entrance to the dancing-floor was crowded with wriggling, hurrying black shapes. The strangeness of being able to see all this that no other living person, except dumb George, had ever seen, thrilled Jarvais deeply. But then suddenly a thought came to him. The sight had made that other both blind and dumb, yet he himself was not affected in the least. What was the reason for this? Its mystery allured him, but he dismissed it from his mind, and sped on after the shadows. He could tell from the way the shadows were moving that the music was now booming on the air, full of hate and lust and darkness. The very thought made him think of those eery fantasmagoria of the Grand Guignol.

They were now at the very threshold of the dancing-floor. Something grasped Jarvais by the shoulders and hurled him through the gateway. Then, hearing a crash behind him that penetrated even through the cotton in his ears, so close he was to it, he turned and saw a huge slab that had fallen from the top of the archway and now lay in the exact centre of the entrance. It seemed to him that the huge stone had an intention—a purpose—a malevolent design. Its fall seemed timed to the fraction of a second. Had it not been for that impetus from unseen forces—had he been but a moment slower—he would have been crushed to pulp beneath its ponderous weight. As he now glanced at it he thought it seemed to have a personality—a soul old and evil—longing to crush to atoms the lives of those who entered its once sacred portals. The mystery of Gilbert's death upon the moor had now been solved: he had been but a moment too late to cross the threshold.

Jarvais swung around again and faced the hard-packed earth of the dancing-floor. Here the shadows were gathered in a ring, circling, whirling to the soundless music, now turning this way, now spinning that, in complete silence, yet in a mad frenzy of motion.

As Jarvais watched them, it seemed as though he were becoming paralysed, and too, something was affecting his eyes—objects became blurred and hazy, yet the shadows themselves became more and more distinct. With a rush the shadows came together, and in a mass. The dance grew wilder and more abandoned.

Suddenly they stopped with shadowy arms uplifted. In the exact centre of the dancing-floor, something was rising; inch by inch it seemed to struggle through the hard-packed earth. Finally, Jarvais could partly distinguish what it was—a huge stone; and by the paleness of the moon, now dimming on the horizon's edge, he could make out its odd shape, which seemed like a monstrous half-moon lying on its back with its two sharp horns pointing skyward. Beside it was another shadow with arms uplifted: that of a man, huge and powerful. Jarvais had never seen a man of such stature. He could see the shadow's giant torso: the swelling chest, the pillar-like legs, and the arms long and muscular with great, long-fingered, prehensile hands—all this cast in high relief against the whiteness of the altar, for altar he now knew it to be. At last the moor had given up to him her deepest secret, and he knew, too, why the search of all but Gilbert had been unsuccessful—and Gilbert had paid with his life for the secret.

The shadow-man lowered his arms and the multitude of shades threw themselves on their faces as the altar finally came to rest on the surface of the floor. To Jarvais it seemed as if thick smoke rolled before his eyes. As through a cloud he saw the shadow-man rise and turn toward him and point a commanding finger. For the first time real terror smote him, and he knew such fear as few men have ever known. He tried to turn and run, but it was as if he were turned to stone as heavy and solid as those silent grey rocks about him. Amid the gathering blackness he saw the shadows, now dimmed, spring suddenly upon him. He felt hot breaths on his cheek. Shapeless, shadowy hands tore at him; strong hands they were. Surely such strength could not belong to bodiless shadows. But he could see no one—just a rolling mass of deeper blackness in the mist before his eyes.

The shadows overbore him and carried him along. Strong arms lifted him up, and now he caught a stench as of something long dead, and of rottenness beyond human ken—yet not dead, but alive, for the dead have no strength, and here was strength abundant. High, high aloft he was lifted; up, up to the altar. The mist that had been before his eyes cleared and he could still feel unseen shadowy hands that tugged at him, pulled at his feet. Up he went, until he could plainly see the fearful carvings on the altar—too horrible even to glance at again. He felt himself wrenched and stretched out and out, and then found himself strung between the horns of the mighty altar.

The moon had almost set, and it was throwing its last dim rays across the plain. Unseen fingers tore the cotton from his ears, and at last he heard what he had dreaded to hear: that uncanny, bestial music of the ruins. It was playing, now softly, now rising in a hellish crescendo, while all about him danced the shadows, noiselessly, ceaselessly. He turned his eyes away and looked up. Towering over him was the tremendous man, or rather the shadow of some giant from the ancient past when the world must have been young and terrible. Stretching his arms toward the dying moon the man knelt. The music ceased with a throb, and the shadows prostrated themselves in a ring about the altar.

The sudden silence beat on Jarvais' frayed nerves more horribly than the din of the music. Long it lasted, this silent prayer to the dying moon, but finally the huge shadow-man arose, reached below Jarvais, and took from its hiding-place a knife. There was nothing shadowy about the knife. It flashed fire in the light and glistened evilly before his eyes. Fascinated, Jarvais watched the shadowy arm lift the crescent blade point-foremost toward the moon, hold it still, then lift it again, now hilt foremost, holding it quivering high in the air. Down came the mighty arm toward Jarvais' chest. He saw it begin slowly—oh so slowly—down, on down—nearer—. Then the moon set, and all was blackness and stillness on the moor.

### [From a London paper]
#### NOTED NOVELIST DISAPPEARS

The mysterious disappearance of Gerald Jarvais, one of England's most noted authors, has caused one of the biggest sensations of the day. Mr Jarvais was spending a week-end at Humbledon on the moors. According to Edward Johnson, the innkeeper, Mr Jarvais had sat in the main room of the inn until late, and then gone to his room. From there he disappeared. His bed had not been slept in, nor had he undressed for the night. Mr Jarvais had no enemies, and the police are unable to find a clue to his whereabouts.

This is the second tragedy of the kind in the little town in as many months. The old wives of the village whisper of strange things on the moor, and say that Jarvais and Gilbert, the man found murdered last month, knew too much about the ruins on the moor. However, the police laugh at such ideas and believe that Mr Jarvais was a victim of foul play. The Authors' League has offered a reward of a thousand pounds for information as to his whereabouts.

# LISHEEN

## *Frederick Cowles*

Frederick Ignatius Cowles (1900–1948) was a librarian who wrote several books on folklore. travel, and Romani culture, as well as the ghost story collections *The Horror of Abbot's Grange* (1936), and *The Night Wind Howls* (1938). During his time as librarian at Trinity College, Cambridge he met M. R. James, who was a strong influence on his early supernatural writings. He was also friends with Dennis Wheatley. His interests in folklore, local history, and the occult, on which he gave lectures, informed many of his short stories. It was these public lectures, for which he would travel the country extensively, which led to ill health and his premature death in 1948. On his death, a further supernatural collection, *Fear Walks the Night*, remained unpublished, although several stories from it were published by Hugh Lamb across his anthologies during the 1970s. In 1993 the collection in its entirety was published by the Ghost Story Press, including the story published here, another early folk horror-esque narrative of pagan rites, stone circles and witches.

Those who know the south-west corner of the Duchy of Cornwall, more especially those who have a taste for ecclesiastical archaeology, will remember with pleasure the lovely little fourteenth century church of St Germal at Germallion.

For many years this delightful building was sadly neglected and allowed to fall into a ruinous condition. The local people were quite indifferent to its decay, for they had little interest in religion. Successive vicars were men of little culture and, even if they had wished to repair the building, could not afford to tackle a job which would obviously prove far beyond their limited means. It is not unreasonable to suggest that, for over two hundred years, the blight of ignorance and superstition depressed this village and turned its inhabitants into a strange, secret community of people who seemed to have no youth.

Then, about the middle of the last century, a change came over the place. The old generation apparently died out completely and men and women from other places took possession of the dilapidated cottages. They brought with them a new spirit and the initiative to make Germallion the tidy village it is today. With the restoration of the Cornish diocese, in 1876, some attempt was made to repair the church, but only essential work was carried out as little money was available.

In 1907 the Reverend John Wheatley was appointed to the living. He was a wealthy man and a learned antiquary, and he immediately set about the colossal task of a thorough restoration. Whilst careful to preserve all the original features of the church, he enriched it with fine screens, statues, and stained glass. Only master-craftsmen were employed in the work and, as a result of their skilled efforts, the building is now as lovely as a page in a medieval Missal. Visitors walk its aisles and admire all they see—excepting, of course, for those few perverted individuals who smell Popery in a whiff of incense and see the influence of sinister Jesuits in every painted saint. A few old tombs remain, but none is particularly interesting. The font is late Norman and came from an earlier church, and there is a magnificent cape chest which has been carefully repaired to hold the modern vestments.

But the greatest treasure possessed by the church is the remarkable set of registers which go back to the year 1592. Antiquaries frequently consult these records but, so far as I know, they have never been transcribed. Some of the more humorous entries have been printed in guide books, but the strangest of them all seem to have been missed or deliberately avoided. Perhaps it has been considered policy to leave them alone for they refer to an episode which is far from edifying. For example, under the date 31st October 1603 can be read:

> Thys daye did I, John Paceye, essay to baptise ye chylde of Minifreda Penryn, deceased, but ye water steamed as yt touched her brow. Yet wyll I save her sowle if thys be possible.
>
> Buryed ye bodye of Minifreda Penryn without ryte or praier for well I know she hath already lost that whych belongeth to God.

For a matter of seventeen years the registers are in the same crabbed hand and contain nothing more exciting than the usual records of baptisms, marriages, and funerals. Then the writing changes with a very peculiar entry dated 23rd June 1620:

On thys daye did the Reverend John Paceye, vycar of thys parysh, vanish from the eyes of mortal men takying with hym that wytch chylde, called Lisheen, to whom he had long synce gyven hys sowle. God grant that he com not agayn.

Little is known for certain of the matter of this John Pacey, although legends of him are still whispered by Germallion firesides on dark winter evenings when the wind howls in the chimneys. In the list of vicars he is given as serving the parish from 1603 until 1620. The Exeter diocesan records contain certain references to the man, and there is a full report into the strange affair of his disappearance. My interest in him was aroused in 1938 when I discovered by chance, in the library of Stirk House in Sussex, a small leather-bound volume which proved to be John Pacey's diary of his years at Germallion. It probably came into the possession of the Cantells through a branch of the family which once owned property in Cornwall. Sir Borlase Cantell kindly permitted me to make a copy of the manuscript, and it was well that I did. In 1942 Stirk House received a direct hit from an enemy bomb and the library, with all its contents, was destroyed.

By a close study of all existing records and my copy of the diary I have been able to reconstruct the curious story of the Reverend John Pacey, vicar of Germallion, who lost his immortal soul for the sake of a witch child.

II

On a day in mid-October 1603 John Pacey rode across the bleak moors beyond Penzance and entered the desolate region known as Germallion Sands. The brooding silence might have depressed an older man. But

Pacey was only twenty-five and journeying to take possession of his first parish. For the two years since his ordination he had been curate at Liskeard and then the Bishop, who was a relative by marriage, had offered him Germallion. The prelate, in a valedictory letter, had hinted that certain difficulties might be encountered by the young man in his new ministry. This is clearly stated in the first entry in the diary which, for the sake of convenience, I shall give in modern English.

He begins with a brief description of the church and rectory, and was apparently well satisfied with both. He goes on: "Sarah Trevaras, who acted as housekeeper to my predecessor, has agreed to serve me in a like capacity. She is a motherly woman and had good fires blazing and a hot meal prepared for me. The village comprises but a hundred or so poor cottages and the people (what I have seen of them) are sullen and unfriendly. The place is encircled by sands which, so legend says, cover a lost city which was destroyed because of the wickedness of its inhabitants. Near at hand to the east is a circle of upright stones which some claim to have been the temple of the lost city. A former vicar wrote much of this stone circle which, he asserted, had a bad influence upon the folk of Germallion. The Bishop, in warning me of possible difficulties, stated that, in his opinion, many of the superstitions of Popery linger in this locality and that witches and warlocks abound."

Now it would seem that soon after his arrival at Germallion, on the 30th day of October to be exact, John Pacey was aroused in the night. "There came to my door," he wrote, "a tall black man who told me that one Minifreda Penryn was sick in childbed and like to die, and that I should hasten to her with all despatch." He made his way to the village and to a cottage where a light shone in the window. There he found a young girl in bed with two old women in attendance. The baby had been safely delivered and, with muttered words, the two crones left the house as soon as the parson arrived. Kneeling by the couch he endeavoured to pray for the dying woman, but found himself unable to utter the usual prayers. He became conscious of the girl's regard and her eyes held a queer mocking light. As he paused in his uncertainty she spoke to him.

"Parson," she said. "Prayers can avail me naught for I go to him who is my true lover and, for his dear sake, I have given my soul to the old gods. Care for my child and you will be rewarded in good time. Fail me in this and I will wreak my vengeance upon you."

"Who is this lover of whom you speak?" cried the dismayed clergyman. "Who is the father of your child?"

A far-away look came into the woman's eyes as she replied, "He came to me in the stone circle which men call Bryn Glas, and his beauty is beyond all mortal loveliness. Soon he will come again to claim me as his bride for all eternity."

The horrified man strove again to stammer the words of a prayer, but his tongue clove to the roof of his mouth and no sound came from his lips. Then, as he knelt there, he heard a mighty wind arise and storm about the cottage. The door burst open and there entered a naked youth, dazzling with an unearthly beauty. The stranger laid his hand for a moment on the head of the new-born babe and then, lifting Minifreda Penryn in his arms, carried her out into the night. John Pacey saw this with his own eyes and he also saw that a dead body lay on the bed as if she, who had been borne away, had no further use for the habiliments of the flesh. A curious music of hellish sweetness filled his ears and, seizing the child, he fled from the house.

Back in the rectory he roused Sarah and bade her attend to the baby. This she was reluctant to do and mumbled much of witchcraft and sorcery. But, knowing in his heart the truth of her whispering, he urged the claims of Christian charity and helped to prepare a cot for the little stranger. It was a girl-child and, as he bent over her, she opened her eyes. He looked into pools of deep green, like matchless emeralds, and saw in their depths things no mortal should behold. Yet in that moment he knew that, for good or ill, their destinies were linked and that he must care for her and keep her under his roof.

In the morning he carried the child to the church intending to baptise her in the Christian Faith and name her Mary. But his tongue refused to utter the sacred words and the drops of water, as they touched the baby's brow, leapt away as if they had fallen upon a live coal. The parson, with a frantic effort, endeavoured to pronounce the formula but not a word could he say. Then another voice, like a soft wind blowing from some secret place beyond the world, whispered the word "Lisheen". Even then John Pacey was not warned, for the green eyes had captured his heart. He carried the child back to the house and took her for his own. Nor did he speak of his inability to administer the sacrament and, to Sarah Trevaras, he said that the girl's name was now Lisheen.

On the day of All Souls he bade the sexton dig a grave and to fetch the body of Minifreda Penryn for interment. All we know of this is the entry in the register and, from that, it is apparent that the parson did not, or could not, carry out the rite of Christian burial. It is not recorded whether any relatives or friends gathered about that unhallowed grave to mourn the dead girl. If any such did attend they were evidently well content that the vicar should have the care of the green-eyed child of Minifreda Penryn.

The diary contains an entry for this day, but it does not refer to the burial.

"After darkness has fallen," wrote John Pacey, "I did chance to look from my window and did see a red blaze in the stone circle on the hill. Then came people hastening through the night. Some hurried on their two legs, but others rode on the air like great birds. All went to that place called Bryn Glas, and I saw their shadows dancing about the fire and heard the music of pipes. As a Christian priest I should have climbed to the temple and denounced their heathen rites. But, God forgive me, I was afraid."

### III

Lisheen, for there was never any doubt about her name, grew in beauty as the years passed, and yet she must have been something of a disturbing influence in the vicar's home. Sarah Trevaras soon became attached to the child and, at the same time, was a little afraid of her. The village accepted her and her position at the parsonage without question. As for the parson himself, he was wrapped up in the girl, and completely under her spell. Yet, from the day of her coming, the heart went out of his work, as if he knew that all his preaching was in vain. The few people who attended the services sat and listened to his discourses with impassive faces. But he soon knew that there was that in their eyes which savoured of half-amused toleration, as if he shared with them some secret which made all his professions of Christianity a hollow sham.

At certain seasons in every year, on the days of the old pagan festivals, he saw the fires blaze in the stone circle and knew that strange and forbidden rites were carried out in the ancient temple. Yet he did nothing to turn the people from their evil ways. In fact, from some of the entries in the diary, it would seem that he was a little envious and, even then, was prepared to share their secret worship.

Lisheen's sixth birthday dawned and, before sunrise, she slipped out of the house and climbed the hill called Bryn Glas. John Pacey, rising with the sun and looking from his window, saw the girl, mother-naked, entering the circle of stones. With feverish haste he donned his clothes and hurried after her calling her name. But she never looked back and, within a few yards of the temple, he found he could advance no further—his feet were chained to the ground. What he witnessed is best told in his own words. "I saw Lisheen, white and beautiful, kneeling at the feet of a tall, dark man who was half-hidden in the shadows. I heard the whisper of strange music and smelt a scent as of rare flowers. How long I stood there I do not know, but suddenly the stranger was gone and I found myself able to enter the circle. Lisheen was still kneeling before a flat stone, like an altar, and by it was a mark in the sand. It was the impression of a cloven hoof."

Pacey escorted the child home and tried to question her as to the reason for visiting Bryn Glas. All she would say was that the time had come when she must know her own people. Soon he knew that on other occasions she climbed to the stone circle and that, when the fires glowed through the night, she danced to the music of the pipes. In his mad folly he did nothing to denounce such wickedness. The only thing that is clear from the rambling entries in the diary is that the girl possessed a wisdom and intelligence beyond her years, and the parson came to regard her almost as a companion of his own age.

Some years after, during the enquiry arranged by the consistory court, it was asserted that, about this time, Pacey ceased to perform the offices of a Christian minister and gave himself entirely to the horned god. An attempt was made to prove that the services held in the church were but blasphemous travesties of religion, and that the Christian altar was used in the abominable rites of Satan. But the only witness brought forward by the accusing parties was a half-demented old woman whose wild statements could not be supported by more reliable people. The diary certainly makes no mention of anything of this nature and, as it is a frank document in every respect, it is unlikely that Pacey would have omitted to record such a vital change in his belief.

In 1615, when Lisheen was twelve years of age, the Archdeacon of Padstow made a visitation of the parish. This dignitary must have given more than cursory attention to the affairs of the place, and yet he reported them as in correct order. He does, however, appear to have resented Lisheen and her presence in the parson's house, and to have corrected her for her seeming precociousness. But it was not until the enquiry of 1620 that he publicly suggested anything in the nature of witchcraft and by then the episode may have been magnified in his mind. In his evidence he stated: "Having cause to reprimand this child, Lisheen, she turned upon me a baneful glance and pointed two fingers towards me. Immediately I was gripped with an agonising pain, as of colic, which doubled me up and tortured my guts for upwards of an hour." It seems strange that, in an age when witch-hunting was all the fashion, the worthy Archdeacon kept this business to himself when he returned from his visitation and did not think it worth recalling until another five years had gone by. Maybe he was influenced by a laudable desire to keep a fellow-cleric free of any suspicion of association with the powers of darkness.

Sarah Trevaras died in the March of 1618 and it is evident from the diary that Lisheen objected to another woman being brought into the house. She undertook to look after Pacey's creature comforts and he seems to have been content with such an arrangement. From that time a new note creeps into the diary. It is dominated by Lisheen. Although she was only fifteen she was a woman in the eyes of the parson, and it is obvious that he was jealous of any who had access to her. He makes frequent mention of the Bryn Glas rites and expresses no proper horror of the pagan ceremonies in which Lisheen, with his full knowledge, regularly participated. There is only a bitter resentment that her body should be exposed for others to see and that he should have no share in those sinful orgies. He writes more and more of her physical attractions—the magic of her eyes, her tempting lips, her graceful beauty. He tells of nights that were bitter with desire. Never once does he record any attempt to cure himself of this obsession, no effort to consult a fellow-clergyman, nor is there any mention of prayer to the God he had vowed to serve. Occasionally he admits that he is afraid. But it is not fear of the divine wrath which causes him any anxiety—only the thought that Lisheen may leave him.

IV

We now come to the year 1620, which brings us to the crisis in this strange affair. The entries in the diary become almost incoherent and it is not easy to follow the story of the final happenings. It would seem that Pacey was already driven almost mad by his desire for Lisheen and that she was only able to restrain him by the promise of satisfaction in the near future. She promised more, for she vowed he should soon be admitted to the secrets of that worship of which she was a votary.

On an April evening he wandered up the hill and into the stone circle. "Suddenly," he writes, "one stood beside me and I saw horns upon his head. And this demon said to me, 'That which you desire shall be yours, but first must you worship me as the lord of the air.' Then I knew that I could struggle no longer and, kneeling down, I adored him and he bade me come to the temple on May Eve."

At the appointed time John Pacey saw the fire blaze in the circle of Bryn Glas and, with his hand in that of Lisheen, climbed the hill. There, if we are to believe the diary, he again did homage to the horned god and was initiated into the secret mysteries. In return he was given Lisheen, but on condition that, when Midsummer came, he should be prepared to follow her into the haunted halls of the lost city and know no more the ways of mortal men.

"In the fierce light of the fires," he wrote, "I held her lovely body in my arms and she gave herself to me. At last she became mine and, for her beauty, I gave my soul."

During those few weeks between May Day and Midsummer no services were held in Germallion church, nor did the people of the village seem to expect their parson to officiate. John Pacey lived only for his Lisheen and yet, in the fulfilment of his desire, he found no satisfaction—nothing more than a burning, all-consuming passion that could not be assuaged.

One who came to the village about that time, and afterwards testified before the consistory court, said: "The vicar appeared as a man in a dream. His eyes must forever be following the witch-child and he was unhappy were she out of his sight but for a moment. I never saw a man so utterly bewitched by the powers of darkness. Sometimes he was afraid and then he would moan, 'Such a little time! Such a little time!' Methinks that, if some godly man could have given him counsel in those days, he might still have saved his soul."

With the approach of the appointed time the parson seems to have lost all interest in life. He shut himself in the rectory with Lisheen and never went abroad. At last the Eve of Midsummer came and the fires of Bryn Glas blazed with a terrible brilliance which was visible from Pendeen in the north and St Leven in the south. The people of those places afterwards said it was a night of fierce storm and that strange figures rode on the wind, as if hastening to some infernal Sabbat. We have no details of what happened on that fatal night. All we know is that the Reverend John Pacey, with his arm around Lisheen, mounted the hill and entered the temple of the old gods. Neither he nor the witch-child were ever seen again in the flesh.

V

The evidence brought before the court of enquiry makes interesting reading and I have already quoted the more important testimonies. The learned divines spent many days in considering the case and eventually the verdict of the court was recorded as follows: "It is our unanimous opinion that John Pacey, vicar of Germallion, was a warlock and unworthy of his sacred calling: that he did vow himself to the service of the master of evil, and did have carnal intercourse with the witch called Lisheen. Therefore, by his own act, he hath cut himself from the Christian communion and, whether living or dead, let him be anathema."

Modern archaeologists tell us that there is, in truth, a city buried beneath Germallion Sands, and that the date of the cataclysm which overwhelmed the place was not less than a thousand years before the Christian era. These savants are of the opinion that Bryn Glas was a temple of that lost land and that its position on the summit of a high hill saved it from being overwhelmed when the city disappeared. Sometimes, when the winds of winter rage and their violence disturbs the sands, fragments of carved stones are revealed. But the spring storms soon move the sands again and the relics are covered before they can be properly examined. Thus nothing is really known of the sinful city which has become a legend of fear in that part of Cornwall.

Often on the dark nights of November, when the candles gleam on the altars of Germallion church and the vested priest chants the Office of the Dead, there comes a sad wailing and a soft tapping on the windows of the sanctuary. The timid ones make the holy sign and dare not raise their eyes from their prayer books. But sometimes one, more daring than the others, looks towards a window in which there is no stained glass and sees, pale against the cold panes, the face of a man who should have been dead long since. And, behind his shoulder, stands a girl of strange beauty whose green eyes shine with the lights of hell.

# THE CEREMONY

## *Arthur Machen*

Arthur Machen (1863–1947), born Arthur Llewellyn Jones in Caerleon-on-Usk, was a journalist, actor, and writer of supernatural, occult and mystical stories. In his works he drew on his background and interests in archaeology and folklore, and he often explored themes of "peri-choresis", which he describes in his short story "N" as "interpenetra-tion", the belief in and experience of a hidden world behind the veil of materialism. The rendering of this veil is key in several of his works, particularly his most famous, "The Great God Pan", and "The White People", the latter of which narrates the tale of a young girl drawn into pagan magic and rituals by her nurse, where, at a secret place in the woods, these practices allow her to encounter the "white people" of the title. The story chosen for this volume was written in 1897 but not published until 1924 when it appeared in the volume *Ornaments in Jade*. It is in many ways a companion piece to "The White People"; here, another young girl recounts her childhood memories of activities in the woods with her nurse, which this time focus on a certain stone in the forest of which she has both a profound fear and a deep reverence.

From her childhood, from those early and misty days which began to seem unreal, she recollected the grey stone in the wood.

It was something between the pillar and the pyramid in shape, and its grey solemnity amidst the leaves and the grass shone and shone from those early years, always with some hint of wonder. She remembered how, when she was quite a little girl, she had strayed one day, on a hot afternoon, from her nurse's side, and only a little way in the wood the grey stone rose from the grass, and she cried out and ran back in panic terror.

"What a silly little girl," the nurse had said. "It's only the... stone." She had quite forgotten the name that the servant had given, and she was always ashamed to ask as she grew older.

But always that hot day, that burning afternoon of her childhood when she had first looked consciously on the grey image in the wood, remained not a memory but a sensation. The wide wood swelling like the sea, the tossing of the bright boughs in the sunshine, the smell of the grass and flowers, the beating of the summer wind upon her cheek, the gloom of the underglade rich, indistinct, gorgeous significant as old tapestry; she could feel it and see it all, and the scent of it was in her nostrils. And in the midst of the picture, where the strange plants grew gross in shadow, was the old grey shape of the stone.

But there were in her mind broken remnants of another and far earlier impression. It was all uncertain, the shadow of a shadow, so vague that it might well have been a dream that had mingled with the confused waking thoughts of a little child. She did not know what she remembered, she rather remembered the memory. But again it was a summer day, and a woman, perhaps the same nurse, held her in her arms, and went through the wood. The woman carried bright flowers in one hand; the dream had in it a glow of bright red, and the perfume of cottage roses. Then she saw herself put down for a moment on the grass, and the red colour stained the grim stone, and there was nothing else—except that one night she woke up and heard the nurse sobbing.

She often used to think of the strangeness of very early life; one came, it seemed, from a dark cloud, there was a glow of light, but for a moments, and afterwards the night. It was as if one gazed at a velvet curtain, heavy, mysterious, impenetrable blackness, and then, for the twinkling of an eye, one spied through a pin-hole a storied town that flamed, with fire about its walls and pinnacles. And then again the folding darkness, so that sight became illusion, almost in the seeing. So to her was that earliest, doubtful vision of the grey stone, of the red colour spilled upon it, with the incongruous episode of the nursemaid, who wept at night.

But the later memory was clear; she could feel, even now, the inconsequent terror that sent her away shrieking, running to the nurse's skirts. Afterwards, through the days of girlhood, the stone had taken its place amongst the vast array of unintelligible things which haunt every child's imagination. It was part of life, to be accepted and not questioned; her elders spoke of many things which she could not understand, she opened books and was dimly amazed, and in the Bible there were many phrases which seemed strange. Indeed, she was often puzzled by her parents' conduct, by their looks at one another, by their half-words, and amongst all these problems which she hardly recognised as problems, was the grey ancient figure rising from the dark grass.

Some semi-conscious impulse made her haunt the wood where shadow enshrined the stone. One thing was noticeable; that all through the summer months the passers-by dropped flowers there. Withered blossoms were always on the ground amongst the grass, and on the stone fresh blooms constantly appeared. From the daffodil to the Michaelmas daisy there was marked the calendar of the cottage gardens, and in the winter she had seen sprays of juniper and box, mistletoe and holly. Once she had been drawn through the bushes by a red glow, as if there had been a fire in the wood, and when she came to the place, all the stone shone and all the ground about it was bright with roses.

In her eighteenth year she went one day into the wood, carrying with her a book that she was reading. She hid herself in a nook of hazel, and her soul was full of poetry, when there was a rustling, the rapping of parted boughs returning to their place. Her concealment was but a little way from the stone, and she peered through the net of boughs, and saw a girl timidly approaching. She knew her quiet well; it was Annie Dolben, the daughter of a labourer, lately a promising pupil at Sunday school. Annie was a nice-mannered girl, never failing in her curtsy, wonderful for her knowledge of the Jewish Kings. Her face had taken an expression that whispered, that hinted strange things; there was a light and a glow behind the veil of flesh. And in her hand she bore lilies.

The lady hidden in hazels watched Annie come close to the grey image; for a moment her whole body palpitated with expectation, almost the sense of what was to happen dawned upon her. She watched Annie crown the stone with flowers, she watched the amazing ceremony that followed.

And yet in spite of all her blushing shame, she herself bore blossoms to the wood a few months later. She laid white hothouse lilies upon the stone, and orchids of dying purple, and crimson exotic flowers. Having kissed the grey image with devout passion, she performed there all the antique immemorial rite.

# THE DARK LAND

## *Mary Williams*

Mary Williams (1903–2000) was a prolific writer of supernatural and ghost stories, publishing over 200 in seventeen collections, the vast majority of which are set in Cornwall, where she moved in 1947. She originally trained as an illustrator at Leicester College of Art. After World War II she illustrated several children's books under the name Mary Harvey, and worked as an illustrator for children's programmes for BBC Wales. As well as her artwork and ghost stories, she also published Cornish-set romance novels under the name Marianne Harvey. The story here, published in *The Dark Land: A Book of Cornish Ghost Stories* (1975), is one of two from that volume that feature stone circles and standing stones—not so surprising given the Cornish setting. "The Trip" is a story of murderous, moving stones, animated through occult-scientific means, while "The Dark Land" is a more subtle tale of the insidious nature of the wild Cornish landscape and its supernatural inhabitants.

The house stands empty now… dark in its hollow, staring with sightless eyes across a tangle of brambles and moorland furze. The stream snakes down from the hill above, and in early summer the bluebells grow thick among the bracken, with thrusting fox-glove and the splash of gorse. A place for mating and nesting surely, for the crying of young things and the shy wild feet of badger and fox. Yet no birds sing there, and the house has fallen into decay. When I knew it those years ago it had a different look; the paint was bright blue against the white walls, and a sun-parlour had been built to the west. This was just after my friends the Carringtons moved in. "Hob's End" they called it, I don't know why. It was Julie's idea. It had been "Four Ways" before… that was when Miss Plummer was there. I had never visited her, but I knew her slightly… a wealthy eccentric, who dabbled in the occult with a young artist living in a cottage nearby. They had become a joke in Port Todric four miles away, where they did their weekly shopping, he carrying her bag, the other arm supporting her, though she was as nimble as a kitten. A doting couple indeed! She even went so far as to launch a book of his verse… etheric stuff in the modern idiom which no one understood.

When he ran off with a barmaid from The Dragon, however, the joke fell flat; for a few days later she was found dead, lying face downwards in the moorland tarn, just beneath the stone, an ancient relic which experts said dated from pre-Druid days. According to the inquest her death had been accidental. But many thought otherwise.

Why was she up there, after all? There was bog quite close; not a place for walking, and she must have known. After that the house was left empty for a year or two. History clung, and folk avoided it. But the Carringtons didn't mind. They were both artists, just married, and the place was exactly what they were looking for.

At that time I was doing a spot of free-lance journalism, and ran over there quite frequently. Julie was elated about the house. After the first few days she had started to paint… vigorous landscapes, full of atmosphere and an exuberant imaginative quality peculiarly her own.

"I shall have an exhibition later," she told me one afternoon when I called for a cup of tea and chat.

"Where? London?"

"Oh, not yet. Port Todric probably… you know, that gallery in Merlyn Street; they let you do that sort of thing now, for a week or fortnight. Not too expensive. I want Ken to join in, but he just won't get down to it."

"Probably feels he's done enough work for a bit," I remarked, "with the decorating and everything."

"Yes," she agreed appreciatively, "he *has* slogged; but it's worth it, don't you think?"

"My word, yes. He's done wonders in this short time. In a way I envy you."

"Only in a way?" she queried.

"Well, it must be rather quiet sometimes. You're quite cut off, aren't you? Still, I suppose that's what you both want."

Her smile faded. "I don't *feel* cut off," she said very quietly. "The country's so *alive* somehow. Always changing you know, exciting, full of moods." Just then Ken came in. He looked a bit tired, I thought, and I told him he should stop the navvying for a while, leave the garden till later. "You've done enough hard labour," I said. "I should have thought you'd want to start a spot of painting with Julie."

"That'll come," he answered. "At the moment she does enough for both of us."

Looking back now I find it hard to pin-point the exact moment of my first unease. It must have been some time in the early autumn, when, as the hills changed from green to gold and deepening russet, Julie's paintings assumed a new quality of tone and intensity. Entangled with the landscape, the strong impression of humped hills, stones, and wind-blown bushes, lurked the suggestion of other things... faces mostly. And yet they had to be found. It was only after some moment's study that they emerged, smiling slyly from the undergrowth and shadowed rocks. A trick of light and shade, I thought at first. But in every painting it was the same. And the faces were not pleasant, or even tangible. That was the worst of it.

"Well, what do you think of them?" Ken enquired one day, as Julie prepared tea in the kitchen. I stared reflectively at the pile of canvases massed along one wall of the studio. "I don't know," I said. "They're unusual, certainly."

Ken laughed shortly. "Oh, come on. Out with it. They're awful, aren't they?"

"Awful?" I said. "I'd hardly say that. Julie can paint. She's no amateur, and they're modern, vigorous; I should say they'll make quite a stir."

"I didn't mean that," he said quietly, "and you know it." When I did not reply, he continued: "Those faces... those awful leering things... Don't tell me you haven't noticed."

"No," I agreed. "They're obvious, I suppose. They weren't at first. But she's got some new idea to flog, and that's how it is. You know Julie... no half measures."

"I *thought* I knew her," he said, "but I'm beginning to think I was mistaken."

"What do you mean? You're happy, aren't you? There's no rift in the marital nest?"

"If there was it would be easier. We could have it out, thrash the thing to a conclusion. Oh no, we don't quarrel. We're not close enough for that any more. It's this painting, John. Ironic, really; it brought us together, and now it's all she thinks about. I wish to God she'd never seen a brush or canvas."

"Come off it," I said. "You don't mean that. You've over tired yourself, and now you're imagining things. This... this craze of hers... it's like a new fashion; it'll wear itself out. You see."

But it didn't. When next I was over Julie was out and Ken was frying something on the stove. She had been gone for the day, he told me, and Heaven alone knew when she'd be back. "It's always happening now," he said. "First thing in the morning, off she goes, and doesn't appear until after dark."

He took me into the sitting room. "Look at this. Have you ever seen anything more... obscene?"

I stared at the canvas before me, cunningly painted with massed shapes resembling rocks and twisted trunks, topped by the stone, standing starkly against a yellow sky which merged subtly into the lurid purples and greens of the tangled undergrowth. Hungry was the word. A hungry vista pulsing with sap and colour; a dark other-world peopled by vile things avid for materialisation. The eyes were there... the greedy lips devised incredibly through line of branch, cloud, and curling stream. Clever, yes. But somehow loathsome.

"Perhaps you should get away for a few days," I suggested. "Why not? You've been here some months now. It would give Julie the chance to..."

"Recover?"

"Get her sense of perspective back. She's gone a bit hay-wire maybe, but fresh surroundings would soon put that right."

"She wouldn't go," he told me. "It's too late."

"Now don't *you* get ideas," I said. "Just put it to her. Tell her it's fixed. That'll do the trick." When he did not reply, I went on: "What about a drink at The Dragon? Leave the eats until later."

"All right," he agreed.

We went down the hill towards the hamlet crouched grey in the valley beyond the road. A thin wind slapped our faces, and the sky was cold with a dying light. There was no sound but the reed-like soughing of the bracken against our legs. Between the writhing fronds I saw the pale malevolent heads of fungi crouched slyly by our feet, peering and sneering almost, like Julie's faces. The ground was damp, sucking where we trod, black and peaty beneath the clutching undergrowth. Hateful somehow. As if sensing my thoughts, Ken remarked: "You feel the same, don't you? I detest this place; and that's putting it mildly."

In the bar of The Dragon, however, he cheered up a little, and later, as we parted to go our different ways, he said: "I guess you're right; I've let things get out of proportion. I'll do what you said... about the change."

But he didn't; because a week later Julie disappeared after going out one afternoon with her sketching materials presumably to paint, Ken apparently had walked about half the night looking for her, and when she had not returned by morning, informed the police. He phoned me from The Dragon as I worked on a spot of copy for the *Penwith Echo*. I finished it off, and drove to Hob's End in my vintage jalopy to discover full details of the business. I expected to find him in a state, but he appeared resigned, almost disinterested. "I knew it would be like this," he said. "For some time I've known. I shall never see her again."

"For Heaven's sake, man," I said, "get hold of yourself. It's crazy to assume the worst. There was a mist last night... she may have taken the wrong track, put up at a cottage or something... or even fallen and

twisted her ankle. She'll be found. Besides... women get ideas sometimes. She's always been a bit... isn't 'fey' the word? Has it occurred
to you that she may just be teasing you?"

"No. Why should she?"

"Why? That's your business. I don't know what goes on between
you two, but it's seemed to me sometimes that you should take a
stronger line. Julie's that kind of woman."

"Julie's been no kind of woman lately," Ken answered shortly.
"Men don't interest her."

"They used to," I remarked drily.

"Once maybe. Not any more."

All that day, and during the week following, an intensive search was
made of the countryside; coast, beaches and moorland were combed,
mine-shafts investigated, and her description issued through radio, press
and television, but with no result. Julie Carrington had disappeared
without a trace... one of those unsolved Cornish mysteries which have
occurred from time to time, stimulating a brief interest, afterwards to
be written off and forgotten.

Ken came and stayed with me for a bit, and in early November put
the house and its contents in the hands of an agent, for sale.

"There's one thing though," he said, when the business was settled.
"Those paintings of hers... I don't want anything done with them."

"You mean you want to keep them?" I asked, surprised.

"Good Heavens, no." He exclaimed: "Anything but. They must
be destroyed. Burnt. We'll have a bonfire, John; it's the only way."

"Are you sure you want that?" I asked. "You never know, someone
might give a good price."

"Yes, I'm sure," he cut in quickly. "I've never been so sure of
anything in my life."

"All right; if that's how you feel."

We set off early the next day with paper and petrol, both of us anxious to get the thing over. The weather was fine and cold, following a night of frost, and Ken remarked that it was an ideal day for a burning. His words chilled me, filled me with unease. Like the old days, I thought, when witches died at the stake. As we climbed the hill wan sunlight streaked the sky, to be shadowed the next moment by leaden clouds blown on the biting wind. Ken shivered, pulling his collar up. "Feels like snow," he said. "God! What a benighted place."

I agreed, but didn't say so. The brambles tore at our legs, and the bracken wailed where we walked with a peculiar dying sound. I felt taut and light-headed from the air, thinking perhaps we should have chosen a calmer day. When we reached the house the sun had quite gone, but the wind tore to the stone above, hissing and whistling round the walls, shrieking in our ears. Ken's hand was shaking when he took off his glove to insert the key. "I couldn't stand much more of it," he said.

"You don't have to," I said lightly. "In a gale like this it should soon be over."

We went inside and collected Julie's paintings. Ken didn't look at them, but just took them one by one to the back of the house, and stacked them into his wheelbarrow. "I hope you're not thinking of a beacon," I said. "It would be some climb up there, and I'm not in Olympic training."

"Just far enough," he said. "By the brook somewhere below the tarn. It'll be blown away from the house up."

We somehow managed to trundle the thing up the slope, and waited there for a breather. "There's just one thing," I reminded him, "in this wind we shall have the whole moor ablaze unless we take some precaution."

So there was nothing for it but to collect stones and erect a wall round the pictures... a kind of circular fireplace which we hoped would be effective. Then Ken poured petrol on the paintings, lit a wad of twisted paper, and dropped it in.

"Get out," I yelled, as the flames shot up. "Watch your step."

We plunged back down the hill and stood watching, while the tongues of fire leaped and danced and twisted tormentedly to the sky, writhing into grotesque shapes of evil... horned shapes curdling into yellowish smoke which billowed and blew towards the bog, where they seemed to pause and quiver, in a stygian green radiance before the screams came... terrible screams above the moaning of the wind.

I knew then where Julie lay, sucked deep into the womb of that evil place. We should never find her; no one would: I remembered Miss Plummer, and village tales of the dark shadow she'd left there. But it was more than that. Miss Plummer had been just another victim, prey of those forces, the elemental evil which had survived with the stone from primeval times, when the bad lands had erupted into birth.

Presently, as the fire died away, I said to Ken: "Come on, let's go."

He took his hand slowly from his eyes and asked: "Did you see it, too?"

I nodded. "It's over now. Forget it."

We never would, of course, not entirely; but in time, I knew, the memory must lose some of its horror.

When we reached the bottom of the hill the sun was out, and the clouds massing away towards the west. The village stood quiet and mellow in the morning light, its church spire tipped with gold.

We both paused, till Ken said: "Let's go in, shall we? It might help."

The church door was open, and as we went through the scent of chrysanthemums drifted from the altar. We knelt down in an ancient pew, and very gradually peace came to us... that peace which is stronger than any force of evil; the one exorcism for the bad things we had known.

# THE MAN WHO COULD TALK WITH THE BIRDS

## A TALE TOLD BY THE FIRESIDE

## *J. H. Pearce*

Joseph Henry Pearce (1856–1909) was a Cornish writer, who published several Cornish-set works in the 1890s, including *Drolls from Shadowland* in 1893 and *Tales of the Masque* in 1894. Both of these received warm reviews in contemporary periodicals but did not seem to have much impact beyond that. *Drolls from Shadowland* in particular is a collection of short supernatural stories firmly based in Cornish folklore, which was described as "a masterpiece" by the *Boston Traveller*, while Pearce was heralded as "a genius at once aerial and intimate" in *The Bookman*. Both simple and poetic, and written in local dialect, "The Man Who Could Talk with the Birds" combines ideas of stone monuments, witches and fairies.

**W**ance upon a time there was a youngster in Zennor who was all'ys geekin'* into matters that warn't no use in the world. Some do say 'a was cliver, too, weth it all, an' cut out that there mermaid in the church† what the folks do come from miles round to see. Anyway, 'a warn't like 'es brawthers an' sesters, an' 'es folks dedn' knaw what to maake of un, like.

Well, wan day when 'a was wand'rin' about, down to Nancledrea or some such plaace, 'a got 'mong lots o' trees an' bushes an' heerd the cuckoos callin' to ayche awther, an' awther kinds o' birds what was singin' or talkin', an' all as knawin' as humans, like. So no rest now cud 'a git, poor chuckle-head! for wantin' to larn to spayke weth they.

Well, it warn't long arter that 'a was geekin' as usual round some owld ruined crellas‡ up to Choon, when 'a seed a man weth a long white beard settin' on wan o' the burrows§ on the hill that are 'longside that owld Quoit¶ up there.

'A was a bowldish piece o' goods, was the youngster, simmin'ly, for

---

\*   Prying.

†   The mermaid, with glass and comb and with the tail of a fish, which is carved on a bench-end in Zennor church.

‡   Ancient hut-dwellings.

§   Barrows.

¶   Cromlech. The term is derived from the legendary belief that these rude megalithic monuments were used by the giants when playing quoits.

'a dedn' mind the stranyer a dinyun,* though 'a *was* like an owld black witch,† they do say. Anyhow, the two beginned jawin' together, an' soon got thick as Todgy an' Tom. An' by-an'-by the stranyer wormed out of un how 'a was all'ys troubled in 'es mind 'cause 'a cudn' onderstaand what the birds was sayin'.

"I'd give anything in the world," says the bucca-davy,‡ "ef I cud onnly larn to spayke weth they."

"Aw, es it so, me dear," said the stranyer: "well, I'll tayche 'ee to talk to they, sure 'nuff, ef thee'll come up to that owld Quoit weth me."

"What must I pay'ee?" axed the youngster, bowld-like. For he'd heerd o' cureyus bargains o' this kind, an' 'a dedn' want to risk 'es sawl.

"Nawthin'! Nawthin', me dear!" said the stranyer. "I shall git paid for't in a way o' me awn."

Well, the end of it was, accordin' to the story, that the youngster 'greed to go 'long weth un: so up the two of 'em went to the Quoit.

When they come up to un the stones seemed to oppen, an' they went inside an' found un like a house. But that was hunderds o' years ago. The owld Quoit now es more like a crellas, though 'a still got a bra' gayte rock for a roof.

Anyhow, they went in, 'cordin' to the story; an' there they lived for a number o' years.

But, somehow, when they was wance got in, the youngster cudn' git out agen nohow. 'A cud geek through the cracks, an' see the country an' the people, but the stones wedn' oppen, an' 'a cudn' git out.

But the owld black witch keeped 'es promise to un, an' tayched un all that 'a wanted to knaw.

---

\* A little bit, in the least.

† In Cornwall *witch* is both masculine and feminine. The *black* witch exercises the most potent magic; the *white* witch being vastly inferior in power.

‡ Fool.

The craws that croaked on the Quoit in the sunshine, an' the sparrers an' wagtails an' awther kinds o' birds that come flittin' round an' cheepin' to ayche awther, the owld witch taughed un ('cordin' to the story) to onderstaand everything any of 'em said.

Well, at laast 'a got so cliver, ded the youngster, that there warn't no bird but what 'a cud talk to; from the owld black raven, wha's all'ys cryin' "*corpse!*" to the putty li'l robins what wedn' hurt a worm.

But aw! lor' Jimmeny! warn't 'a disappointed when 'a found what 'a'd ben so hankerin' arter warn't wuth givin' a snail's shill to knaw.

He'd ben thinkin', 'fore 'a cud onderstaand them, that what they'd be talkin' about to ayche awther wed be somethin' cureyus an' mighty cliver, all sorts o' strange owld saycrets, s'pose. But 'a found, when 'a come to spayke their language, that instead o' tellin' 'bout haypes o' treasures, an' hunted housen, an' owld queer ways, they was all the time talkin' 'bout their mait or their nestes, an' awther silly jabber like that.

So 'a was mighty disappointed, an' got very law-sperrited, though 'a dedn' like to confess it to the witch.

An' now, thinks the youngster, he'd like to go home agen: an' shaw off 'fore the nayburs, s'pose.

"Well, thee cust go," says the owld witch, grinnin'.

"An' what must I pay'ee for tayching' me?" says the youngster.

"Nawthin', sonny! Nawthin' at all!" says the witch. "I shall git me reward in a way o' me awn."

An' weth that 'a bust out laughin' agen.

Well, anyway, the lad, accordin' to the story, wished un "*good-bye,*" an' trudged off home.

But aw! poor dear! when 'a got to Zennor 'a nigh 'pon brok 'es heart weth grief.

He'd ben livin' all alone weth the owld black witch, an' 'a hadn' took no note of what was passin', an' 'a thought 'a was still a youngster, simmin'ly: 'stead o' which 'a was graw'd to an owld, owld man, weth no more pith in 'es bones than a piskey; an' 'a cud hardly manage to crawl to Zennor, 'a was so owld an' palchy*, an' nigh 'pon blind.

An', wust of all, when 'a got to Zennor everywan who knaw'd un was dead an' gone! 'Es faather an' mawther was up in the churchyard, an' 'a hadn' got a single friend in the world!

So because 'a was so owld an' terrible palchy, an' hadn' got nowan to taake no int'rest in un, through never havin' took no int'rest in nowan, they was obliged to put un up to Maddern Union; an' there 'a lingered, owld an' toatlish,† 'tell 'a died at laast a lone owld man.

---

*    Weak.
†    Silly.

# THE STONE THAT
# LIKED COMPANY

## *A. L. Rowse*

A. L. Rowse (1903–1997) was primarily a historian, who gained his degree from Oxford, becoming the first Fellow of All Souls College from a working-class background. He was later a lecturer at the London School of Economics. He specialised in Elizabethan England, and is credited with identifying the "dark lady" of Shakespeare's sonnets. During his prolific career, he also focused considerably on his native Cornwall, and published several autobiographical pieces about his Cornish childhood, as well as poetry and history.

*West-Country Stories* was published in 1945, and was described in *Publishers' Weekly* as an "unusual collection of stories and essays of the supernatural, of antiquarian lore, and of echoes of the long ago". Rowse himself described the stories as narratives of both fact and fiction, in that "the stories of invention, even though mostly ghost stories, have a foundation of fact; while the narratives of fact, I hope, are not wholly without imagination". The story published in this volume—about a longstone, which folklore has imbued with a sacrificial history, and a young boy's obsession—involves this co-mingling; in Rowse's book *The Little Land of Cornwall* (1986), he describes how the titular stone of the story was based on a menhir in a field next to his former house at Polmear Mine, St Austell, which was once known as Tregeagle's Walking Stick (and now is referred to as the Gwallon Longstone).

I t was the Christmas vacation: and those few Fellows who were still up—happy to see the backs of their undergraduates and to be quit of the dreary routine of lectures and tutorials for a blessed five weeks—had foregathered that evening, after a quiet common-room dinner, in the rooms of the Dean. The Dean, in spite of his name, was a secular, a very secular person; his inclinations were hospitable, indeed he was rather overmuch given to entertaining. Though he had the cold, wary eyes of an intelligent fish, he was in fact a jovial person, not happy unless he had one or two of his friends in after dinner to sip his admirable port.

Tonight they were five: four of them drinking port and one—the wisest of them—with his glass of burgundy. This last was just raising his glass to his lips, when suddenly the lights went out. In itself no remarkable, nor that winter infrequent, circumstance; for it had happened several times of late that there had been a breakdown at the electric light works from which the college current came. The winter was a severe one; floods had broken out by the river and the works flooded. There was no knowing how long before the light would come on again.

Patient men, sitting heavy after a substantial meal, they sat there for a moment, their faces lit up momentarily by the gleams from the oak-log burning in the grate. Then the Dean rose, fetched out of the corner cupboard two pleasant little candlesticks, lit them and placed them on the mantelpiece: their flame, when it caught up, revealed their pretty Regency pattern, a single column with a wreath of foliage running round the stem.

"Hadn't somebody better tell a story?" said the Economics don: a hearty man with rubicund face and white sweater to match. He had a knack of saying what everybody thought.

"Yes, let's tell sad stories of the death of kings," said the English don, a young man who had only recently joined the college.

"Well, who's got a story to tell?" said the Dean.

The general opinion was that he had; indeed he was well known for his stories. As host he couldn't very well have declined, even if he had wanted to. It was a situation he loved, for his inclination was all in favour of a story—his own story, and himself telling it.

"Well, since you will have it—" he began, settling himself well into the back of his chair, his head between the two side flaps in deep shadow, looking more than ever like some queer extinct animal with large flapping ears, while from the depths gleamed those intelligent eyes behind the spectacles. "There's a house in Cornwall that I know—" he went on.

"Oh! come, Mr Dean," said the Economics don, who knew well the Dean's penchant for old houses in Cornwall haunted by ghosts.

"Well, as a matter of fact, it's not that kind of house at all," said the Dean, quite unperturbed. "It's a modern house, built after the last war. In fact, it's a bungalow, or what I believe is called a semi-bungalow. Some friends of mine took it for a bit some years ago, perhaps as much as fifteen years ago—how time flies! *Pereunt et imputantur*. They took it for a bit. They didn't stay there long." He paused, dug further into the back of his chair, hugging himself, then resumed.

"I said 'friends of mine': but really it was the widow of a friend of mine and her son, a delicate lad, liable to asthma and bronchitis, and that sort of thing. He was very highly strung, I gather, but intelligent and extremely sensitive—at any rate, he was as a child, the only time that I saw him. The mother took this house in Cornwall for the benefit of his health because of the climate. The climate agreed with him; it wasn't the climate that—"

"What was it?" said the eager young English lecturer, not used to the Dean's roundabout way of telling a story.

"Just you wait, young man," said he, not at all put out. "The house was ideal from their point of view: not too large, very convenient, and could be run with one servant and a man in occasionally to look after the garden. My friend, Mrs Wilford, took a great deal of interest in it. Not so the boy: perhaps it would have been better for him if he had.

"His hobby was antiquities. He was just about the age when boys are mad about archaeology, would go chasing off on his bicycle to take rubbings of brasses in Cornish churches and all that sort of thing. Probably did him no good: he was a restless, inquiring sort of lad who could never take things easily. There was always an element of over-strain about him. I suppose he must have been eighteen or nineteen: he would have been up here if it hadn't been for his health. I'm not sure that he wasn't a good deal spoiled by his mother: her only child, and he being rather an invalid. He was good-looking, too, like his father: I saw a photograph of him after—well, after what happened. He had that striking combination of jet-black hair with deep-blue eyes which you sometimes come across in Scots people. He was tall and rather overgrown. There was a curious fanatic look in his eyes. He had another passion, too, besides archaeology—music. He would sit for hours listening to concerts on the wireless—in those early days of wireless. He was beginning to compose, too: not very professional, perhaps, but he certainly had a streak of something, more than talent.

"It so happened that a couple of fields away from the house there was a longstone: one of those megaliths which you get in Cornwall and

Ireland—this was a particularly fine specimen. The Devil's Walking-stick, the local people called it: they have some story about how it came to be there—you know the kind of thing. It is there no longer. After what happened—"

There was a movement of impatience on the part of the eager young man. The Dean poured himself out a second glass of burgundy in leisurely fashion.

"Well—some of the young miners thereabouts got together one night and blew it up."

"What?" said the Classics don in a tone of horror: he was himself interested in archaeology in a mild way. "An interesting megalithic monument like that, destroyed by these vandals only a few years ago? I've never heard of such a thing. How did it come to happen? Of course, we all know that in previous centuries when people didn't value these things, didn't know what they were, they sometimes broke them up and used them for gate-posts on their farms, or for road-stone."

"How do you know that they didn't know what they were doing?" said the Dean, with an odd tone in his voice. His eyes had a curious intense look in them. "That they meant to break it up, and did it deliberately? They might have been *afraid*"—he underlined the word significantly with his smooth voice—"and even though they were afraid, they nevertheless went through with it. I call that courage of a sort.

"You wouldn't have heard of it," he resumed in his ordinary speaking voice, with no suggestion in it. "Nothing was said about it in public. All the local people were in it: they knew who had done it all right. But they never would say; for they all wanted it done. And I think," he said, fixing the Classics don with his eyes, "after you have heard what I am going to tell you, you will agree that they were not without reason.

"Of course it was an enormous attraction to the house in young Christopher's eyes when he first discovered the stone. He took it as if he were its first discoverer—'silent upon a peak in Darien' and that sort of thing—would he had been, poor lad!

"As a matter of fact, he could get nothing out of the local inhabitants about the stone or its history. They knew nothing about it—or said they knew nothing about it. In itself sufficiently curious when you come to think of it, for it was an exceedingly fine one. Young Christopher himself took its measurements. He found that it was over nine feet above ground: that meant that there must have been at least four or five feet more buried in its socket underground. At its broadest it was about two feet nine inches; it had a curious shape, for beneath the head the stone was, of course, unhewn; it had not, so far as one could tell, been shaped by human hands—all the same it gave the impression, a very strong one, of having a head slender and pointed. But beneath the head it broadened out noticeably on one side like a huge mis-shapen shoulder, rather threatening in appearance.

"Christopher was wildly anxious to dig round it, expose the socket if possible, and see what he could find. He never mentioned it to anyone—nobody seemed to be interested. It never occurred to him to ask permission of anyone—least of all of the stone," the Dean added quietly.

"One autumn afternoon—there was nobody about much on that part of the coast—he started operations upon the socket. It was all very enthusiastic and unwise: if he had been successful and got on far enough with it he might have loosened the stone sufficiently for it to have toppled over—perhaps on to him. But he didn't get so far as that. He had no experience of digging or of professional archaeology: he was just the enthusiastic amateur. You will agree, my dear Done," he said, addressing the historian among them, who had so far not spoken, was in fact struck by the story, which touched a chord in his experience—"you will agree that there is no more dangerous person—even though the danger is more to himself than to others." The Dean leaned forward, took up his glass from the little mahogany wine-bracket by the fireside, sipped two mouthfuls of burgundy, and went on.

"Young Christopher didn't as a matter of fact get very far with his digging operations. It was a pleasant enough day when he set out across the intervening fields, with their magnificent view of the bay spread out beneath in a kind of shelving curve; for the stone stands—or rather stood—in a splendid natural situation overlooking the bay. In primitive days before the coppices and plantations thereabouts had been laid out, and when all the fields were open downs, an uncultivated moor, it must have been a dominating object on the skyline from the coast below: a long forefinger pointing heavenwards, perhaps a propitiatory object, no doubt the centre of the religious cult of the primitive people round about, almost certainly the scene of human sacrifice with its attendant rites.

"The boy had not been long at work, heaving up the earth feverishly, in a frantic state of excitement—very bad for him—when there came on, as happens in Cornwall at that time of year, a sudden change in the weather. The sky was quickly filled with lowering grey cloud, which cast a cold uncomfortable atmosphere upon the scene—you know that sinister grey half-light than which there is nothing more cheerless in the world, or more sinking to the spirits. You might have felt a sensation of well-being and contentment a moment before, and then this dark cloud comes down upon you like a weight of lead. From being a warm afternoon it became suddenly cold; and very soon there followed a stiff shower of hail, for shelter from which Christopher ran to the heavy stone hedge, such as you have in the West Country. While sheltering there he was struck by the changed appearance of the stone. Whether it was that he was cowering down for shelter from the blast, it seemed to him that the stone had grown enormously larger. He noticed how it looked exactly to the west and the setting sun, and the thought of primitive sacrifice came into his mind. He almost fancied that he could see the blood running into the groove that he had exposed, hear the demented shrieks of the gibbering throng in that

Home of the silent vanished races,

like the innumerable mammering of bats' voices in the air. There was something horrible in the threatening headlessness of the stone, the shapelessness that was yet suggestive of power, of a ruthless natural force imprisoned in it incapable of expressing itself, or of any release. Suddenly, terrified, he could bear it no longer. But he was a lad of courage and he was too proud to take to his heels. He withdrew in good order, even going so far as to retrieve his pick and shovel, but having the feeling that he was fighting a rear-guard action all the way out of the field and over the hedge. It was the end of his digging operations. He had had a scare—even if it had been possible to resume, which it was not; for the hail shower was the prelude to a blizzard, which very unwontedly snowed them up for a week or two. It was the stone that resumed operations, in its own way, in its own time."

There was a pause. A coal fell from the fire into the grate. The Dean leaned forward and put another log on, which burned up brightly, lighting up the intent faces of his colleagues. He sank back into the shadows. You could hear the soft ticking of his tiny clock in its Chippendale case, with the little lion's head handles, on the mantelpiece.

"The scare that he had had did not put the boy off. It might have been better if it had. I repeat that he was a lad of courage, like his father; though very excitable and nervous, he had spirit. The scare only increased his fascination for the stone: he longed to know more about it, to get to the bottom of it. He was determined to go on—you know the way such boys have of never letting sleeping dogs lie, they won't let a thing alone when it's better it should be—even if that stone had been a sleeping dog and prepared to be left alone.

"During those weeks of snow and sleet and slush"—

> (Fire and fleet and candle-lighte
> And Christe receive thy saule

—the words ran through the mind of the young English don)—"very exceptional for Cornwall," commented the prosaic mind of the Dean, "Christopher got to work to read everything he could lay hand on that might give him some information. He began naturally with Carew's *Survey of Cornwall*—his father had had a copy of the very pleasant 1769 edition. He drew a blank: nothing whatever about the stone. He went on to all the other old histories of Cornwall, Polwhele, Borlase, Davies Gilbert. Borlase's *Natural Antiquities of Cornwall* did mention the stone and its position, but gave no further particulars.

"However, his reading was not without some effect, for he gathered two bits of information which enabled him to piece together a picture of the district in primitive times in his mind. Less than a mile away, towards the other end of the bay, was a farm called Castle Dennis. There was a stile-field just above the farm, with a path leading across it which cut off a roundabout corner going by the road. After you left the field by the second stile, you found yourself deep in a little lane leading to the third. It was a favourite walk of his. For some reason the field had got the name 'the Field of the Dead' in his mind. It always had a curious intimate feeling for him: 'Campo dei Morti' he would say over to himself crossing it, and one day he wrote a poem about it in which occurred the line—

So many dead men have made this their home.

But it had never occurred to him, what now he learned from these old authorities, that that field actually was the inside of a primitive camp, that the little lane into which you descended was the deep ditch or foss outside the rampart; that the name Castle Dennis was a corruption of the old Celtic *dinas*, meaning fortress. He learned, too, that at the other end of the bay, not far from the longstone, there had been a series of barrows which had been broken into in the eighteenth century and robbed of their funeral urns with their contents of charred human bones.

"The whole picture of the district as it was in primitive times came clear in his mind. There at the other end of the bay had been their encampment, their town, for centuries: there was even a little cliff castle down upon the headland for refuge in time of danger, in those dangerous days when life was so precarious. At the opposite end of the bay was the town of the dead, the cemetery with its barrows where they buried the burned bones of their chieftains. Near the latter was the longstone, the centre of their worship with its fearful barbarous rites.

"In a fever of excitement he read on and on in those weeks. From works on Cornwall he turned to books on stone-age Britain, on the megalithic period, on megalithic religion, on Avebury and Stonehenge. It made a strong, an unforgettable impression when he read that when the altar-stone at Stonehenge was excavated they had found the cleft skull of an infant, evidently a dedicatory sacrifice. He could not forget it. Still his mind raced on and on, forgetting everything else, putting on one side his music, poetry—neglecting everything for the sake of this passion, this morbid fascination.

"At the same time his reading had made him very knowledgeable about the history of the locality. When some local female society—I think it was a Women's Institute—kept badgering his mother to go and lecture to them, his mother, who was a very shy and timid woman, let him go and take her place. He promised he would give them a lecture on the history of their parish—very bold of him, but he had the temperament for it, and what with his enthusiasm and good looks it was a great success. Of course it was all, or mainly, about the longstone and the portrait of the district in primitive times that he had constructed in his mind. He told them that here was one of the finest megalithic monuments in the county—by far the oldest historical monument in the district—and nobody seemed the least proud of its possession or even interested in it. One had never even heard of its existence. Oughtn't it to be put on the map, etc.? He ended by asking them for any information they had about it, any stones connected with it. The audience did not seem to take the subject up with any enthusiasm; they were more interested in him. He was too young to note that in fact they rather sheered off it, and quite deftly—though in the manner of Cornish people purely instinctively—they succeeded in deflecting him from it.

"But a day or two later when walking in the vicinity he ran into a woman who stopped him and talked to him about the subject. She was an odd sort of woman, rather masculine in type with a way of swinging to and fro on her hips as if she were a sailor. She was, as a matter of fact, the wife of the captain of a vessel, and prided herself on the fact: so perhaps she got the habit from him. She came close up to the young man, putting her face into his—he stepped down off the pavement unobtrusively into the gutter to give her room.

"'By the way, Mr Wilford,' she said, 'you won't know me. My name is Mrs Chynoweth. But I was very interested by the lecture you gave to our institute the other day. You spoke of the old longstone over there in the field. Well, I remember Mr Coombe who used to live in the farm just below, and his family before him for a hundred years back;

and he used to say that there was a tradition that somebody had been executed there—oh, hundreds of years ago. I don't mean executed just like that, you know—'

"'You mean—human sacrifice?' said Christopher; somehow there flashed across his mind what he had read of somewhere, the picture of some poor creature left out on a last outpost of rock facing the setting sun, with a loaf of bread and a pitcher, the tide around those islands rising higher and higher.

"'Yes, that's it,' she said, rolling her fine dark eyes at him and revealing her powerful dentures in a broad smile. 'And I remember,' she went on, 'when we were children in the village we never used to play in that field. Nobody ever did, or went into it if they could help it.' She moved nearer to him, like an old man of the sea whom he couldn't shake off even if he would; though he was in fact fascinated. 'Have you ever noticed how threatening it looks with that great heavy shoulder, crouching like somebody ready to lurch out at you?' She made the motion expressively with her heavy body. Christopher moved a shade further away. 'Just as if they were waiting to attack you,' she said.

"Christopher did not encourage these suppositions; they made all the greater impression upon him.

"'Are you interested in spiritualism?' she said, and without waiting for an answer continued, 'Well, I am. And once in London when I went to a spiritualist church and they asked for questions, I thought I'd ask about this old longstone and whether it had any influence upon people's lives round about. The answer came that I was psychic, and should keep away from such things: they are liable to exert a sinister influence on you.'

"Deviating into egoism, released and unashamed, she ceased to be interesting. Christopher found some halting excuse, took his leave, and went on his way.

"His way took him back along the coast by the path that skirted the field where the stone was. From the shelter of the hedge he could observe the figure, as it were without being observed. There was no doubt it bore an extraordinary resemblance to the figure of a hooded and shrouded woman. The great bulging shoulder might be a child it was carrying, that it had taken in its arms for some purpose, draped and veiled. But it was the very formlessness of it, the shaped shapelessness, the fact that headless it seemed to have a head, shoulderless and armless it seemed to have shoulders and arms, or at least on this side shoulder and arm; the blankness of it, standing there through the centuries looking to the west with unseeing eyes, a blind face to the setting sun, that made it at once so terrible and so pathetic. For tonight he could see its pathos, its loneliness, the embodiment of grey despair, deserted for centuries by its votaries, living its own terrible secret life, the embodiment of imprisoned force.

"Greatly affected by the spectacle and his own teeming imaginings, he hurried by. Yet when he crossed the gap of the gate, from which he could be observed, he could not but feel a distinct tremor run through his nerves. Greatly daring, he turned back for a last look. The stone looked quite different: a bar of angry light from the west rested upon its upper face: it looked blank, impersonal, menacing.

"Christopher had been pestering his mother for days to come and visit the stone with him, wanted to have the name of the house changed to Longstone House, so great was his mania on the subject. At last, not in the least interested, she went along with him to pacify him. That same evening he quarrelled bitterly with her. It was their first (and last) quarrel: they had never so much as bickered before. But that night Christopher, led on by what impulse, uttered things to his mother—about his father, for example, whom he scarcely remembered—such as had never even entered his head before. It was as if a preternaturally old experience of life had suddenly been injected into his veins.

"From that moment everything began to go wrong. As if he had some presentiment of this and of how things would end, he began to keep secretly a journal of the terrible experience that he was to undergo. Later, his mother sent it to me, and after her death it remained in my possession.

"Rarely can a lad of his years have endured such hallucinations—if hallucinations they were that led to such an indubitable result.

"From the eastern windows of the house, where Christopher's bedroom was on the ground floor, the longstone was visible, as I have said, across a couple of intervening fields. It seems that the lad got the sense that he was being ceaselessly watched. One night as he was going to bed late, as his habit was, his nerves on edge, he drew back the curtains to peer out. What he saw there in the moonlight, very lovely and unearthly upon the snow, made him draw back in terror. There was no sleep for him that night; he fancied he had seen the stone—which, as you know, was a couple of fields away—as large as life, as if it were on watch outside his window.

"Of course, it was just the disordered fancy of a child. He said not a word of what he suffered, but wrote down what he at any rate was convinced of in the journal he kept. But he never slept in that room again. It was shut up. He moved upstairs to a little attic room under the roof, with a dormer window that looked to the west.

"Nothing happened any more for a few days. He fancied he was safe. He took his mind off his obsession and turned to his music. He began to forget the scare he had had. It is dangerous to forget.

"One night he went to have a bath before going up to bed. The bathroom was at the back of the house and looked to the north. There was just enough light for him to see, and he was lying full length humming some theme that had occurred to him that evening, trying it out various ways in his head, when he looked up casually to see a long gaunt finger of shadow resting upon the window from outside. He turned cold with horror. Grabbing his dressing-gown he fled upstairs to the safety of his room.

"But now he knew that he was no longer safe wherever he was. The bathroom looked to the north; the longstone stood in the fields to the east of the house. He could no longer console himself with the thought that it was an hallucination. He longed to leave the house; he hated the thought of the shadow that lay upon it and about it, that laid siege to it on every side. But he was afraid—afraid to confess that he was afraid, and so held on.

"The very next day he ran into Mrs Chynoweth out walking again.

"'You don't seem to look very well,' she said in her breezy, familiar way. She was dressed as usual in dark heavy tweed with a man's soft felt hat worn slightly on one side. She carried a walking-stick with which she executed little cuts in the air; she was jauntier than ever. 'Cornwall not agreeing with you, perhaps? I shouldn't wonder, not in that house of yours with the name it's got with people here.'

"'What name?' said Christopher, surprised into indiscretion. So far as he was aware it was simply known as 'The Bungalow'.

"'Oh, people here call it "Longstone House". Didn't you know what happened there a year or two ago with the last tenants who had the house? They didn't tell you when you took it? No, of course not. People are so secretive about things; I can never understand why. Now I'm different; I'm open; I believe in being candid.'

"She certainly did. She didn't need Christopher's apprehensive invitation to tell him what had happened before plunging into her story.

"'Well, it was very nasty for the time,' she said, 'and that was why the house stood empty until you came. There was a very nice couple that built the house just after the war. They came down here from London with their little girl. She was about ten or eleven—yes, eleven, the same age as my little girl. One evening just as it was getting dark she went down the drive to the gate—you know, where the path leads out into the road that comes from the longstone. She was found there a little later. They missed her from the house, and when they went down the drive there she was lying just outside her own gate. It was supposed that she had been knocked down by a passing lorry. But nobody had seen one. Nobody here believed that it was a lorry that was responsible. When they picked the poor little thing up, her right shoulder was shattered and there was a fracture of the right temple: just as if she had been lurched into by something very heavy. And believe me, it wasn't a car that did it.

"'Now I don't know if you are interested in spiritualism, Mr Wilford—'

"Christopher did not need her assurance, and the thought of her philosophising on the subject after what he had been through himself was more than he could bear. He took to his heels and unashamedly fled back to the house.

"That night alone he sat up late to listen in to a concert he particularly wanted to hear, for it included the Fourth Symphony of Sibelius, the most monolithic of them all. He shut himself in the dining-room of the house, a room with heavy brocade curtains across the big window that looked due south. He had his journal out before him, into which he poured his soul: all his fears, agonies, all the things he felt he could share with no one: all written in pell-mell as if he had no time to spare—nor had he, poor lad!—mixed up with musical themes jotted down, which he was trying out for some work that he wanted to compose—there was the title: 'Campo dei Morti'.

"As he listened, everything seemed to become unnaturally clear to him; there was the inevitability of fate in the great marching strides of the basses in the first movement, very low, menacing steps coming nearer and nearer, which nothing could stop. In all this stony waste of sound, no tenderness, no sweetness, until at the moment of sacrifice the flutes sounded clear like human voices, wringing a certain sweetness out of the very stone, the heart of stone. Then there came the shrill insistent lament of violins, that pathetic motif of protest against the menacing rhythm of those monolithic steps. As he listened and wrote, his nerves on edge, a sixth sense rather than any reason told him that the moment had come, that the long striding steps of the basses in the music led in the world of space out through the window, that beyond the curtains there was that waiting for him to which all his brief life had been a pilgrimage. In short, if he tore open the curtains there would be the stone waiting for him.

"He could bear the suspense no longer, but flung back the curtains, threw open the window—at least that's the way it seems he must have gone—rushed down the drive to the gate, the way the little girl had gone before him, and along the path to where the stone awaited him. It would seem that that stone had a hunger for what was young and innocent.

"It was not until the early hours of the morning that they found him, lying like a sacrificial offering at the foot of the socket he had ventured to uncover. His right shoulder was crushed and the whole right side of his face was bruised and grazed as in some embrace that had been too strong for him. They found him in the grey light of a morning moon: an old moon, a rind of a moon upon its back in the west, which turned the whole landscape into death's kingdom and lit his face with a strange glimmer there where it lay at the stone's foot."

The Dean's story had come to an end. His eyes shone with an unusual intensity, as if he were more concerned by it than he cared to admit. Just before the end the electric light had come on again, with something of a shock; so that the end of the story had been told in the hard glitter of unaccustomed light in their eyes, while the candles wavered their rather ghostly light on the mantelpiece. Nobody said anything for a moment. Then the young English don recited half aloud, half to himself:

> This ae nighte, this ae nighte,
> —Every nighte and alle,
> Fire and fleet and candle-lighte,
> And Christe receive thy saule.

Shortly afterwards, with a few brief words and Christmas greetings, they dispersed severally to their beds.

# MINUKE

## *Nigel Kneale*

Most famous for his ground-breaking TV dramas such as the *Quatermass* series, Nigel Kneale (1922–2006) was primarily raised on the Isle of Man before moving to London in 1946 to study at RADA. In 1948 he published his collection of macabre stories, *Tomato Cain*, for which he won the prestigious Somerset Maugham Award. From here he focused exclusively on writing as a career, becoming a staff writer at the BBC, a cinema producer, and later a writer with ITV. During this time he forged a successful partnership with producer Rudolph Cartier and created some of the most memorable TV work of the twentieth century, including the *Quatermass* series (1953–1979), the six-part horror anthology *Beasts* (1976), and the TV play *The Stone Tape* (1972). In the latter, stone is the medium for the horrors that follow, a theme which previously appeared in the story chosen here. Originally published in *Tomato Cain*, "Minuke" combines ancient superstition with modern technology, to terrifying results.

The estate agent kept an uncomfortable silence until we reached his car. "Frankly, I wish you hadn't got wind of that," he said. "Don't know how you did: I thought I had the whole thing carefully disposed of. Oh, please get in."

He pulled his door shut and frowned. "It puts me in a rather awkward spot. I suppose I'd better tell you all I know about that case, or you'd be suspecting me of heaven-knows-what kinds of chicanery in your own."

As we set off to see the property I was interested in, he shifted the cigarette to the side of his mouth.

"It's quite a distance, so I can tell you on the way there," he said. "We'll pass the very spot, as a matter of fact, and you can see it for yourself. Such as there is to see."

It was away back before the war (said the estate agent). At the height of the building boom. You remember how it was: ribbon development in full blast everywhere; speculative builders sticking things up almost overnight. Though at least you could get a house when you wanted it in those days.

I've always been careful in what I handle—I want you to understand that. Then one day I was handed a packet of coast-road bungalows, for letting. Put up by one of these gone tomorrow firms, and bought by a local man. I can't say I exactly jumped for joy, but for once the things looked all right, and—business is inclined to be business.

The desirable residence you heard about stood at the end of the row. Actually, it seemed to have the best site. On a sort of natural platform, as it were, raised above road level and looking straight out over the sea. Like all the rest, it had a simple two-bedroom, lounge, living-room, kitchen, bathroom layout. Red-tiled roof, roughcast walls. Ornamental portico, garden strip all round. Sufficiently far from town, but with all conveniences.

It was taken by a man named Pritchard. Cinema projectionist, I think he was. Wife, a boy of ten or so, and a rather younger daughter. Oh—and dog, one of those black, lop-eared animals. They christened the place "Minuke," M-I-N-U-K-E. My Nook. Yes, that's what I said too. And not even the miserable excuse of its being phonetically correct. Still, hardly worse than most.

Well, at the start everything seemed quite jolly. The Pritchards settled in and busied themselves with rearing a privet hedge and shoving flowers in. They'd paid the first quarter in advance, and as far as I was concerned, were out of the picture for a bit.

Then, about a fortnight after they'd moved in, I had a telephone call from Mrs P. to say there was something odd about the kitchen tap. Apparently the thing had happened twice. The first time was when her sister was visiting them, and tried to fill the kettle: no water would come through for a long time, then suddenly squirted violently and almost soaked the woman. I gather the Pritchards hadn't really believed this—thought she was trying to find fault with their little nest—it had never happened before, and she couldn't make it happen again. Then, about a week later, it did: with Mrs Pritchard this time. After her husband had examined the tap and could find nothing wrong with it, he decided the water supply must be faulty. So they got on to me.

I went round personally, as it was the first complaint from any of these bungalows. The tap seemed normal, and I remember asking if the schoolboy son could have been experimenting with their main stop, when Mrs Pritchard, who had been fiddling with the tap, suddenly said, "Quick, look at this! It's off now!" They were quite cocky about its happening when I was there.

It really was odd. I turned the tap to the limit, but—not a drop! Not even the sort of gasping gurgle you hear when the supply is turned off at the main. After a couple of minutes, though, it came on. Water shot out with, I should say, about ten times normal force, as if it had been held under pressure. Then gradually it died down and ran steadily.

Both children were in the room with us until we all dodged out of the door to escape a soaking—it had splashed all over the ceiling—so they couldn't have been up to any tricks. I promised the Pritchards to have the pipes checked. Before returning to town, I called at the next two bungalows in the row: neither of the tenants had had any trouble at all with the water. I thought, well, that localised it at least.

When I reached my office there was a telephone message waiting, from Pritchard. I rang him back and he was obviously annoyed. "Look here," he said, "not ten minutes after you left, we've had something else happen! The wall of the large bedroom's cracked from top to bottom. Big pieces of plaster fell, and the bed's in a terrible mess." And then he said, "You wouldn't have got me in a jerry-built place like this if I'd known!"

I had plasterers on the job next morning, and the whole water supply to "Minuke" under examination. For about three days there was peace. The tap behaved itself, and absolutely nothing was found to be wrong. I was annoyed at what seemed to have been unnecessary expenditure. It looked as if the Pritchards were going to be difficult— and I've had my share of that type: fault-finding cranks occasionally carry eccentricity to the extent of a little private destruction, to prove their points. I was on the watch from now on.

Then it came again.

Pritchard rang me at my home, before nine in the morning. His voice sounded a bit off. Shaky.

"For God's sake can you come round here right away," he said. "Tell you about it when you get here." And then he said, almost fiercely, but quietly and close to the mouthpiece, "There's something damned queer about this place!" Dramatising is a typical feature of all cranks, I thought, but particularly the little mousy kind, like Pritchard.

I went to "Minuke" and found that Mrs Pritchard was in bed, in a state of collapse. The doctor had given her a sleeping dose.

Pritchard told me a tale that was chiefly remarkable for the expression on his face as he told it.

I don't know if you're familiar with the layout of that type of bungalow? The living-room is in the front of the house, with the kitchen behind it. To get from one to the other you have to use the little hallway, through two doors. But for convenience at meal-times, there's a serving-hatch in the wall between these rooms. A small wooden door slides up and down over the hatch-opening.

"The wife was just passing a big plate of bacon and eggs through from the kitchen," Pritchard told me, "when the hatch door came down on her wrists. I saw it and I heard her yell. I thought the cord must've snapped, so I said, 'All right, all right!' and went to pull it up because it's only a light wooden frame."

Pritchard was a funny colour, and as far as I could judge, it was genuine.

"Do you know, it wouldn't come! I got my fingers under it and heaved, but it might have weighed two hundredweight. Once it gave an inch or so, and then pressed harder. That was it—it was *pressing* down! I heard the wife groan. I said, 'Hold on!' and nipped round through the hall. When I got into the kitchen she was on the floor, fainted. And the hatch-door was hitched up as right as ninepence. That gave me a turn!" He sat down, quite deflated: it didn't appear to be put on. Still, ordinary neurotics can be almost as troublesome as out-and-out cranks.

I tested the hatch, gingerly; and, of course, the cords were sound and it ran easily.

"Possibly a bit stiff at times, being new," I said. "They're apt to jam if you're rough with them." And then, "By the way, just what were you hinting on the phone?"

He looked at me. It was warm sunlight outside, with a bus passing. Normal enough to take the mike out of Frankenstein's monster. "Never mind," he said, and gave a sheepish half-grin. "Bit of—well, funny construction in this house, though, eh?"

I'm afraid I was rather outspoken with him.

Let alone any twaddle about a month-old bungalow being haunted, I was determined to clamp down on this "jerry-building" talk. Perhaps I was beginning to have doubts myself.

I wrote straight off to the building company when I'd managed to trace them, busy developing an arterial road about three counties away. I dare say my letter was on the insinuating side: I think I asked if they had any record of difficulties in the construction of this bungalow. At any rate I got a sniffy reply by return, stating that the matter was out of their hands: in addition, their records were not available for discussion. Blind alley.

In the meantime, things at "Minuke" had worsened to a really frightening degree. I dreaded the phone ringing. One morning the two Pritchards senior awoke to find that nearly all the furniture in their bedroom had been moved about, including the bed they had been sleeping in: they had felt absolutely nothing. Food became suddenly and revoltingly decomposed. All the chimney pots had come down, not just into the garden, but to the far side of the high road, except one which appeared, pulverised, on the living-room floor. The obvious attempts of the Pritchards to keep a rational outlook had put paid to most of my suspicions by this time.

I managed to locate a local man who had been employed during the erection of the bungalows, as an extra hand. He had worked only on the foundations of "Minuke," but what he had to say was interesting.

They had found the going slow because of striking a layer of enormous flat stones, apparently trimmed slate, but as the site was otherwise excellent, they pressed on, using the stone as foundation where it fitted in with the plan, and laying down rubble where it didn't. The concrete skin over the rubble—my ears burned when I heard about that, I can tell you—this wretched so-called concrete had cracked, or shattered, several times. Which wasn't entirely surprising, if it had been laid as he described. The flat stones, he said, had not been seriously disturbed. A workmate had referred to them as "a giant's grave," so it was possibly an old burial mound. Norse, perhaps—those are fairly common along this coast—or even very much older.

Apart from this—I'm no diehard sceptic, I may as well confess—I was beginning to admit modest theories about a poltergeist, in spite of a lack of corroborative knockings and ornament-throwing. There were two young children in the house, and the lore has it that kids are often unconsciously connected with phenomena of that sort, though usually adolescents. Still, in the real-estate profession you have to be careful, and if I could see the Pritchards safely off the premises without airing these possibilities, it might be kindest to the bungalow's future.

I went to "Minuke" the same afternoon.

It was certainly turning out an odd nook. I found a departing policeman on the doorstep. That morning the back door had been burst in by a hundredweight or so of soil, and Mrs Pritchard was trying to convince herself that a practical joker had it in for them. The policeman had taken some notes, and was giving vague advice about "civil action" which showed that he was out of his depth.

Pritchard looked very tired, almost ill. "I've got leave from my job, to look after them," he said, when we were alone. I thought he was wise. He had given his wife's illness as the reason, and I was glad of that.

"I don't believe in—unnatural happenings," he said.

I agreed with him, non-committally.

"But I'm afraid of what ideas the kids might get. They're both at impressionable ages, y'know."

I recognised the symptoms without disappointment. "You mean, you'd rather move elsewhere," I said.

He nodded. "I like the district, mind you. But what I—"

There was a report like a gun in the very room.

I found myself with both arms up to cover my face. There were tiny splinters everywhere, and a dust of fibre in the air. The door had exploded. Literally.

To hark back to constructional details, it was one of those light, hollow frame-and-plywood jobs. As you'll know, it takes considerable force to splinter plywood: well, this was in tiny fragments. And the oddest thing was that we had felt no blast effect.

In the next room I heard their dog howling. Pritchard was as stiff as a poker.

"I felt it!" he said. "I felt this lot coming. I've got to knowing when something's likely to happen. It's all round!" Of course I began to imagine I'd sensed something too, but I doubt if I had really; my shock came with the crash. Mrs Pritchard was in the doorway by this time with the kids behind her. He motioned them out and grabbed my arm.

"The thing is," he whispered, "that I can still feel it! Stronger than ever, by God! Look, will you stay at home tonight, in case I need—well, in case things get worse? I can phone you."

On my way back I called at the town library and managed to get hold of a volume on supernatural possession and what-not. Yes, I was committed now. But the library didn't specialise in that line, and when I opened the book at home, I found it was very little help. "Vampires of south-eastern Europe" type of stuff. I came across references to something the jargon called an "elemental" which I took to be a good deal more vicious and destructive than any poltergeist. A thoroughly nasty form of manifestation, if it existed. Those Norse gravestones were fitting into the picture uncomfortably well; it was fashionable in those days to be buried with all the trimmings, human sacrifice and even more unmentionable attractions.

But I read on. After half a chapter on zombies and Rumanian werewolves, the whole thing began to seem so fantastic that I turned seriously to working out methods of exploding somebody's door as a practical joke. Even a totally certifiable joker would be likelier than vampires. In no time I'd settled down with a whisky, doodling wiring diagrams, and only occasionally—like twinges of conscience—specu-lating on contacting the psychic investigation people.

When the phone rang I was hardly prepared for it.

It was a confused, distant voice, gabbling desperately, but I rec-ognised it as Pritchard. "For God's sake, don't lose a second! Get here—it's all hell on earth! Can't you hear it? My God, I'm going crazy!" And in the background I thought I was able to hear something. A sort of bubbling, shushing "wah-wah" noise. Indescribable. But you hear some odd sounds on telephones at any time.

"Yes," I said, "I'll come immediately. Why don't you all leave—" But the line had gone dead.

Probably I've never moved faster. I scrambled out to the car with untied shoes flopping, though I remembered to grab a heavy stick in the hall—whatever use it was to be. I drove like fury, heart belting, straight to "Minuke," expecting to see heaven knows what.

But everything looked still and normal there. The moon was up and I could see the whole place clearly. Curtained lights in the windows. Not a sound.

I rang. After a moment Pritchard opened the door. He was quiet and seemed almost surprised to see me.

I pushed inside. "Well?" I said. "What's happened?"

"Not a thing, so far," he said. "That's why I didn't expect—"

I felt suddenly angry. "Look here," I said, "what are you playing at? Seems to me that any hoaxing round here begins a lot nearer home than you'd have me believe!" Then the penny dropped. I saw by the fright in his face that he knew something had gone wrong. That was the most horrible, sickening moment of the whole affair for me.

"Didn't you ring?" I said.

And he shook his head.

I've been in some tight spots. But there was always some concrete, actual business in hand to screw the mind safely down to. I suppose panic is when the subconscious breaks loose and everything in your head dashes screaming out. It was only just in time that I found a touch of the concrete and actual. A kiddie's paintbox on the floor, very watery.

"The children," I said. "Where are they?"

"Wife's just putting the little 'un to bed. She's been restless tonight: just wouldn't go, crying and difficult. Arthur's in the bathroom. Look here, what's happened?"

I told him, making it as short and matter of fact as I could. He turned ghastly.

"Better get them dressed and out of here right away," I said. "Make some excuse, not to alarm them."

He'd gone before I finished speaking.

I smoked hard, trying to build up the idea of "Hoax! Hoax!" in my mind. After all, it could have been. But I knew it wasn't.

Everything looked cosy and normal. Clock ticking. Fire red and mellow. Half-empty cocoa mug on the table. The sound of the sea from beyond the road. I went through to the kitchen. The dog was there, looking up from its sleeping-basket under the sink. "Good dog," I said, and it wriggled its tail.

Pritchard came in from the hall. He jumped when he saw me.

"Getting nervy!" he said. "They won't be long. I don't know where we can go if we—well, if we have to—to leave tonight—"

"My car's outside," I told him. "I'll fix you up. Look here, did you ever 'hear things'? Odd noises?" I hadn't told him that part of the telephone call.

He looked at me so oddly I thought he was going to collapse.

"I don't know," he said. "Can you?"

"At this moment?"

I listened.

"No," I said. "The clock on the shelf. The sea. Nothing else. No."

"The sea," he said, barely whispering. "But you can't hear the sea in this kitchen!"

He was close to me in an instant. Absolutely terrified. "Yes, I have heard this before! I think we all have. I said it was the sea: so as not to frighten them. But it isn't! And I recognised it when I came in here just now. That's what made me start. It's getting louder: it does that."

He was right. Like slow breathing. It seemed to emanate from inside the walls, not at a particular spot, but everywhere. We went into the hall, then the front room: it was the same there. Mixed with it now was a sort of thin crying.

"That's Nellie," Pritchard said. "The dog: she always whimpers when it's on—too scared to howl. My God, I've never heard it as loud as this before!"

"Hurry them up, will you!" I almost shouted. He went.

The "breathing" was ghastly. Slobbering. Stertorous, I think the term is. And faster. Oh, yes, I recognised it. The background music to the phone message. My skin was pure ice.

"Come along!" I yelled. I switched on the little radio to drown the noise. The old National Programme, as it was in those days, for late dance music. Believe it or not, what came through that loudspeaker was the same vile sighing noise, at double the volume. And when I tried to switch off, it stayed the same.

The whole bungalow was trembling. The Pritchards came running in, she carrying the little girl. "Get them into the car," I shouted. We heard glass smashing somewhere.

Above our heads there was an almighty thump. Plaster showered down.

Half-way out of the door the little girl screamed, "Nellie! Where's Nellie? Nellie, Nellie!"

"The dog!" Pritchard moaned. "Oh, curse it!" He dragged them outside. I dived for the kitchen, where I'd seen the animal, feeling a lunatic for doing it. Plaster was springing out of the walls in painful showers.

In the kitchen I found water everywhere. One tap was squirting like a fire-hose. The other was missing, water belching across the window from a torn end of pipe.

"Nellie!" I called.

Then I saw the dog. It was lying near the oven, quite stiff. Round its neck was twisted a piece of painted piping with the other tap on the end.

Sheer funk got me then. The ground was moving under me. I bolted down the hall, nearly bumped into Pritchard. I yelled and shoved. I could actually feel the house at my back.

We got outside. The noise was like a dreadful snoring, with rumbles and crashes thrown in. One of the lights went out. "Nellie's run away," I said, and we all got into the car, the kids bawling. I started up. People were coming out of the other bungalows—they're pretty far apart and the din was just beginning to make itself felt. Pritchard mumbled, "We can stop now. Think it'd be safe to go back and grab some of the furniture?" As if he was at a fire: but I don't think he knew what he was doing.

"Daddy—look!" screeched the boy.

We saw it. The chimney of "Minuke" was going up in a horrible way. In the moonlight it seemed to grow, quite slowly, to about sixty feet, like a giant crooked finger. And then—burst. I heard bricks thumping down. Somewhere somebody screamed.

There was a glare like an ungodly great lightning-flash. It lasted for a second or so.

Of course we were dazzled, but I thought I saw the whole of "Minuke" fall suddenly and instantaneously flat, like a swatted fly. I probably did, because that's what happened, anyway.

There isn't much more to tell.

Nobody was really hurt, and we were able to put down the whole thing to a serious electrical fault. Main fuses had blown throughout the whole district, which helped this theory out. Perhaps it was unfortunate in another respect, because a lot of people changed over to gas.

There wasn't much recognisably left of "Minuke." But some of the bits were rather unusual. Knots in pipes, for instance—I buried what was left of the dog myself. Wood and brick cleanly sliced. Small quantities of completely powdered metal. The bath had been squashed flat, like tinfoil. In fact, Pritchard was lucky to land the insurance money for his furniture.

My professional problem, of course, remained. The plot where the wretched place had stood. I managed to persuade the owner it wasn't ideal for building on. Incidentally, lifting those stones might reveal something to somebody some day—but not to me, thank you!

I think my eventual solution showed a touch of wit: I let it very cheaply as a scrap-metal dump.

Well? I know I've never been able to make any sense out of it. I hate telling you all this stuff, because it must make me seem either a simpleton or a charlatan. In so far as there's any circumstantial evidence in looking at the place, you can see it in a moment or two. Here's the coast road...

The car pulled up at a bare spot beyond a sparse line of bungalows. The space was marked by a straggling, tufty square of privet bushes. Inside I could see a tangle of rusting iron: springs, a car chassis, oil drums.

"The hedge keeps it from being too unsightly," said the estate agent, as we crossed to it. "See—the remains of the gate."

A few half-rotten slats dangled from an upright. One still bore part of a chrome-plated name. "MI—" and, a little farther on, "K."

"Nothing worth seeing now," he said. I peered inside. "Not that there ever was much—Look out!" I felt a violent push. In the same instant something zipped past my head and crashed against the car behind. "My God! Went right at you!" gasped the agent.

It had shattered a window of the car and gone through the open door opposite. We found it in the road beyond, sizzling on the tarmac. A heavy steel nut, white-hot.

"I don't know about you," the estate agent said, "but I'm rather in favour of getting out of here."

And we did. Quickly.

# NEW CORNER

## L. T. C. Rolt

L. T. C. Rolt (1910–1974) was a professional engineer, who wrote copious volumes on Britain's industrial heritage and transportation systems. He was a pioneer of canal preservation, living on a narrow boat after the Second World War, and setting up the Inland Waterways Association with Robert Aickman in 1946. Alongside this, he also published supernatural short stories, many of which were collected in the 1948 volume *Sleep No More: Twelve Stories of the Supernatural*. When it was re-issued by Branch Line in 1974, it was given the new subtitle of *Railway, Canal, and Other Stories of the Supernatural*. As may be inferred, these stories drew heavily upon Rolt's industrial background. The story presented here was originally published in 1937 in *Mystery Stories* magazine and is set in the world of car-racing, but even the thoroughly modern setting cannot overcome the vengeful spirits of an ancient stone circle.

**T**he Blighs were late as usual, and practice day was nearly over when their familiar old Vauxhall with its loaded trailer rumbled into the paddock.

It was the first meeting of the 1938 season at the famous Longbury Hill, and promised to be the best of a long series, for the enthusiastic organisers, the Mercia Motor Club, had been preparing for the event as never before. Not only had they managed to secure an international date for the first time, but they had improved the hill out of all recognition, widening, re-surfacing and constructing one entirely new section of road. These efforts had been justly rewarded by what was probably the finest entry list that a speed hill climb in this country had ever produced.

Germany had sent over one of her Grand Prix Rheinwagens—a 3-litre, 16-cylinder, rear-engined job—to be handled by no less a person than Von Eberstraum himself. France had entered her most successful driver, Camille, with Monsieur Rene Lefevre's latest masterpiece, a double-cam straight-eight of conventional design—somewhat untried, but a joy to the eye, like all Rene's cars. Most noteworthy of all, Italy was to be represented by her veteran "Maestro", Emilio Volanti, driving a marque which had not been associated with his name for some time, a 3-litre Maturati, the first Italian car seriously to challenge German speed supremacy.

The British reply to this formidable Continental opposition was provided by the works team of B.R.C.'s, and a host of sprint "specials".

The former were smaller than their Continental rivals, but the course suited them and, with the exception of the new section, their drivers had the advantage of knowing the hill intimately.

The "specials" were, as always, an unknown quantity. Some, on their day, were quite capable of matching the performance of the Grand Prix cars over such a short course, while others might merely provide comic relief by emitting remarkably irregular noises and bestrewing the course with intimate parts of their machinery.

There was no doubt about it, the stage was set for a record meeting. No wonder Mr Nelson, the genial little secretary and moving spirit of the M.M.C., had felt excited and pleased with himself that morning when he had watched lorries bearing names famous on all the circuits of Europe come rolling into his paddock.

Brothers Peter and John lost no time in unloading the Bligh Special from its trailer.

"If you go and rout out the Scrutineer," said Peter, as they man-handled the Special into its bay, "I'll go and talk nicely to Nelson and see if I can't wangle one run before dark."

John had barely finished unloading from the tonneau of the Vauxhall, the cans of dope, the tools and all the other paraphernalia that accompanies the sprint car, when Peter came back at the double.

"It's Okay," he called. "But we shall have to hurry; Nelson's send-ing over the Scrutineer. Meantime, we've got to go for a walk, blast it! All drivers have got to go over the new section on foot and report to the timing-box that they've done so before they're allowed a run." He paused, peering round the paddock. "I wonder where those silly asses can have got to? I told them to keep a look-out for us," he complained.

"Maybe they've got fed up with waiting and gone off to the Crown," John hazarded.

"I'll half break their silly necks if they have," Peter swore. "No, there they are snooping around the Maturati. Oi!" he bellowed. "Mike! George!"

Two tall, untidy figures detached themselves from the curious group about the Italian car and came towards them at a jog-trot.

"Where the hell have you been?" shouted one as soon as he came within earshot. "We'd just given you up—thought you must have thrown the trailer away again on the way, so we were just going to make for the local taphouse."

"Never mind about that now," Peter silenced him. "Your thirst will improve with keeping. The great thing at the moment is to get a practice run before dark. John and I have got to walk over the new bit of the course, so if you'd like to make yourself really useful for a change, you can get her ready and warmed up while we're away. That's the dope-can, the one with the white top. It's all ready mixed. The soft plugs are in, but you'd better have a look at them before you try a start. When she's just about sizzling, put in the R2s, they're in that yellow box. Oh, and another thing," he added, "the Scrutineer is on his way, so none of your rudery or he may take a poor view of John's idea of independent suspension."

"As you say, Chief," Mike replied with mock humility, and pulled his forelock. Yet he took his coat off and set to work with a will, ably assisted by the quiet George, while the others set off up the course.

Whereas the old road wound its way up through the wood in a series of zigzag curves, thus gaining height on an easy gradient, the new section left the old at the first of these corners, and cut straight and steeply up the hillside for a distance of 300 yards to a single left-handed turn. This was followed by another straight on a slightly easier gradient, which ran parallel with the flank of the hill until it rejoined the old course, at what had previously been the very slow Creek Hairpin.

Peter and John stood on the apex of the new corner, surveying it with critical and practised eyes.

"There's no doubt about it, this is a great improvement," John decided.

"It'll make the course much faster and more interesting, too. This 'swerve' reminds me of the first bend of the 'esse' at Shelsley; same gradient up to it, I should think, same curvature and camber, and the same bank on the outside, too, for the unwary to clout.

"Of course, it's difficult to judge just how steep that approach is, so that one can't tell exactly where the cut-off point will be, but I should say it will be just about opposite those stones there."

He pointed to two great boulders that stood like monoliths, one on each side of the road. Peter nodded.

"I think you're right," he agreed. "It looks straightforward enough and yet—oh, I don't know—there's something I don't like about it, but exactly what it is I couldn't tell you. Phew!" he exclaimed and laughed shortly, "what a stink! Old socks and rotten eggs aren't in it. Something must have died here a long time ago I should think."

"That's funny," said John, sniffing. "I don't notice it. Anyway, we'd better get down, it seems to be getting dark all of a sudden under these trees, so unless we hurry we shan't have enough light for a run."

When they got back to the paddock practically everyone had packed up for the night, but the faithful Mike and his shadow George had the Special ready and only awaiting a push to the line. Peter wriggled his way into the narrow bucket-seat in front of the two potent "Vee" twin engines and the others pushed.

Letting in the clutch he was greeted with the deafening staccato bark of four open exhausts belching blue flame and a reek of dope and castor-oil. For a few moments the air about the timing-box was filled with an intensity of urgent sound that literally stung the ear-drums to painful protest, while Peter tightened his body-belt, pulled down his goggles and exchanged a last shouted word or two with John.

Then at a nodded signal Mike released the plungers of the two oil-pumps and stepped back, the note of the engines rose even more fiercely, and the next instant the car was snaking out of sight in a series of power slides, leaving in its wake two long, black streaks of pungent burnt rubber from the tyres.

"A bit too much loud pedal there," Mike commented.

Although invisible to him, John could follow Peter's progress by the noise that now resounded through the wood and echoed about the surrounding hills. Now he had cut-out and changed down for the first corner into the wood—a sharp one that—now he was round and accelerating away for all he was worth up the steep straight to the new corner; he was through to second, now into third—that was a surprise, he had not expected that Peter would get into third. Now he had cut-out for the new corner.

John waited expectantly for a renewed burst of sound, but no sound came. He must have crashed. Then, after what seemed an age of suspense, but must in reality have been but a second or two, he heard the sound of one engine come to life and continue over the top of the hill. John heaved a sigh of relief and walked round to meet the car at the foot of the return road; anyway, Peter and the Special were still in one piece.

Peter came coasting back in a fine fury, consigning with great fluency the M.M.C., the hill, the local inhabitants, and the new corner to a particularly lurid hell. John gave him a few moments in which to simmer down before he dared to enquire what had happened.

"What happened?" Peter exploded with renewed fury. "Well, I was going a treat, as you probably heard. Pulling third on the straight, too, when just as I came into the new corner some suicidal idiot came flapping out at me waving his arms plumb in the middle of the road. It meant that I had to brake and alter course right in the middle of the corner, and it was no fault of his that I didn't pile up the whole outfit. As it was, I just touched the bank on the outside, shot across the road, went up on the grass on the inside and eventually managed to get back on to the road again. By that time one engine had cut out; still, I think the car's all right. We shall have to get up bright and early and get in a couple of runs tomorrow morning, that's all, there's not enough light in the wood for another run now."

When the Blighs eventually arrived at the Crown in Winchford where they had arranged to stay, they found Mr Nelson leaning on the bar, chatting to Camille and Butt, the number one B.R.C. driver. He looked up and smiled as they came in.

"Well, how did you get on, Bligh?" he enquired.

Peter grinned ruefully.

"Oh, all right, thanks, as far as it went, which wasn't very far, I'm afraid."

"You're not going to tell me you had trouble on the new corner, are you?" Mr Nelson implored. "Everyone seems to have been in difficulties there. I've heard nothing but complaints about it all day. The surface, the camber, the light—nothing seems to be right about it. It's pretty disheartening for me after so much work. Even Volanti said he had a nasty moment there, although he put up an excellent time. Three people have hit the bank, fortunately without serious damage, and several others had their engines die quite unaccountably when they came to open up after the corner." Mr Nelson looked quite downcast.

"Oh, no," Peter hastened to assure him. "I've got no complaint to make against the corner itself, but just as I came into it some fool popped out from nowhere right into the middle of the road, waving his arms like a lunatic. Result was, I had a very busy time indeed, and while I was motoring about on the grass and dodging trees I lost one engine."

Poor conscientious Mr Nelson looked more harassed than ever and swore under his breath.

"I'm most frightfully sorry to hear about this, Bligh," he apologised. "I can't think who can have done such a crazy thing. When you went up, the marshals had just come down and reported to me that there were no spectators left on the hill, and only Arthur Day was still up there, hanging on in the top timing-box until you had made your run. Tell me, what did this idiot look like?"

Peter thought for a moment before replying.

"Well," he explained, "the light was pretty poor under the trees there by the time I went up, and anyway you can't notice much detail when you're 'dicing', but he seemed a tall, thin bloke wearing something white. It looked like an overall coat, or it may have been a very light-coloured mackintosh.

"The odd thing that struck me, now I come to think of it, was that he didn't seem to have the coat on properly—his arms through the sleeves I mean—but slung round his shoulders, so that it looked like—well—more like a surplice than anything else."

He laughed.

"I'm not trying to suggest, though, that it may have been the local padre in his war-paint or anything like that. Just as I got the car back on to the road," he went on, "I had a quick look round, but he must have made a lightning getaway, for I couldn't see a sign of him. Anyway," Peter concluded, "I'm not worrying, it was my own fault for turning up so late. What'll you have to drink?" he asked.

The conversation became general and the usual topics that are raised on the eve of a speed event were discussed at length. Talk was of blowers and blower pressures, of gear ratios, suspension and braking systems and of twin rear wheels versus single.

Mr Nelson played his part nobly in this discussion, for he was secretly a prey to a vague feeling of uneasiness, a dim sense of foreboding, which began to get the upper hand later, when he found himself alone in his room for the night. That confounded new corner seemed to be at the bottom of everything, he reflected; what an unlucky job it had been from start to finish! A constant worry. At one time he had seriously doubted whether the road would ever be ready in time, they had had such a long chapter of accidents and irritating annoyances.

In the first place, the local wiseacres had been even more pigheaded and obstinate than usual, and had not only refused to help the work of the club in any way, but had actually seemed bent on putting obstacles in their path. None of the local contractors could be persuaded to take on the job, and he had been compelled to employ a London firm at much greater expense. All this because of some archaic superstition about a ring of old stones through which the road would pass.

To begin with, some foolish practical joker, presumably one of the villagers, kept moving the surveyor's pegs and sights overnight, and once they had even been collected together and burnt. Next, a large oak-tree they were felling, thanks to an unexpected and violent gust of wind on an otherwise calm day, fell unexpectedly in the wrong direction. It trapped the foreman, seriously injuring him, while several of the men had narrow escapes.

The mechanical navvy broke down repeatedly, until finally a subsidence occurred beneath it, and it required days of digging and the erection of shear-legs before it could be extricated. Just when the excavations were nearly at an end, and they were preparing to lay the foundations of the road, a spring had been struck, which made the whole hillside a hopeless quagmire of mud.

Then the trouble began among the workmen. Several of them fell victims to a peculiar and singularly unpleasant complaint, from which two had subsequently died, and the remainder had become restless and uneasy, saying there was no luck on the job. No doubt local talk was responsible.

Seeing the work was so behind time, he had tried to persuade the contractor to put on a night shift, offering to provide them with flares, but the men had resolutely refused to work after sundown. It was only by the dogged persistence of Mr Nelson himself that the road had been completed in time for the event, and it was with a sense of personal triumph that he had opened the course to competitors.

When beset by all these difficulties, he had actually begun to wonder at times whether there might not, after all, be some truth in local superstitions, but when the new road was at last finished and he toured up it at the wheel of his blue saloon Le Fevre, this disturbing thought had been forgotten. Now, the unfortunate mishaps in practice and particularly Bligh's story had recalled his past uneasiness.

He recollected how he had dismissed impatiently the workmen's talk of something or someone flitting about among the trees; never seen in broad daylight, but only after sundown, often glimpsed in the corner of the eye, but never directly seen. Strange, too, that both workmen and drivers had complained of the unpleasant stench that occasionally seemed to hang about the corner.

In an attempt to put a stop to these disquieting and unprofitable thoughts, Mr Nelson decided to indulge in his favourite relaxation of reading in bed. After a while the book slipped from his hand on to the coverlet and he fell into an uneasy sleep, which brought with it a very vivid and disturbing dream.

He was sitting in his favourite position in the lower timing-box at Longbury. It was evidently late in the day, for the light seemed subdued. Through the window he could see the Rheinwagen on the starting-line with Von Eberstraum at the wheel. For no apparent reason this perfectly normal spectacle seemed to inspire him with dreadful uneasiness. He felt as though he was the unwilling witness of some sinister sequence of events which he was quite powerless to interrupt.

He saw the starter place the contact shoe before the front wheel of the car, and as he did so a voice said quite clearly and distinctly, "He's out for blood."

Then the Rheinwagen made its anticipated meteoric getaway. Mr Nelson realised that he had the headphones on, and listened anxiously for the reassuring voice of Arthur Day to announce the time. It did not come.

Instead his head became filled with a distant but penetrating reverberation of sound. It was like nothing he had ever heard before, but it most closely resembled the far-off booming of a great gong. Then a thin, high voice began to intone in a tongue that was unintelligible, and yet somehow indescribably menacing. Finally, and seemingly much nearer at hand, someone screamed.

At this point Mr Nelson awoke with the scream still ringing in his ears, to find himself bathed in perspiration, despite the fact that he had kicked most of the bedclothes on to the floor. Disinclined to court further sleep that night, and feeling wretchedly ill at ease, he propped himself upright with his pillows and resigned himself to read his novel, with as much concentration as he could muster, for the rest of the night.

A brilliant spring morning without a cloud in the sky did much to dispel Mr Nelson's gloomy fears and to make amends for his wretched night. He felt inclined to attribute his nightmare to over-indulgence in the Crown's excellent Stilton at dinner the previous evening.

When he opened the course at noon, accompanied by the President of the Club and a minor Royalty, he felt in excellent humour once more. A record crowd of spectators thronged the banks and enclosures on the hill and the fields below were black with cars.

In the interval between the first and second runs Mr Nelson felt justified in laughing at his forebodings, for the unfortunate incidents of practice day had not re-occurred, and the programme had been run off like clockwork. It was obvious that the honour of fastest time of the day lay between Von Eberstraum and Volanti with the Maturati. Von Eberstraum, it appeared, had a slightly faster car, but he held an advantage of a mere fifth of a second over Volanti, who was handling his car with that almost fabulous skill for which he was justly famous.

A brilliantly judged climb by Butt in No. 1 B.R.C. won him first place in the 1½-litre class, and third in the general classification, while the Bligh Special had made an ear-splitting run to record the fastest time by a sprint "special". The performance of the new Lefevre was a little disappointing, and Camille could only manage fifth place. Mr Nelson could see him in the paddock now, explaining volubly and with a wealth of gesture typically Gallic, to a group of equally vociferous mechanics, why the car was quite useless and unfit for him, the great Camille, to drive.

It was just as the first car was being brought to the line for its second run that an unfortunate and most unusual mishap occurred to delay the proceedings. Without any warning a section of the bank above the new corner gave way and slid down into the road, carrying several spectators with it. Fortunately no one was injured, and amidst much laughter and jesting a gang of amateur navvies was hastily recruited, and set to work with a will to clear the earth on to the inside of the corner. Even so, the delay caused was such that Mr Nelson realised that unless the rest of the programme was run off extremely promptly, the light would fail the last cars.

However, once the obstruction had been cleared and the spectators moved back as a precautionary measure, the second runs were made amidst much excitement, but again without untoward incident. Von Eberstraum and Volanti both made faster, but this time identical times, and sent a message to the timing-box requesting that they be allowed an additional run each to decide the tie. This was granted, though the two drivers were urged to come to the line as soon as possible on account of failing light. The announcement that the tie was about to be run off provoked a murmur of excited anticipation and speculation from the dense crowds on the hill.

Volanti appeared first, as the Rheinwagen mechanics were changing rear wheels. As he was pushed to the line and the engine of the Maturati was started the sun was just sinking beyond the horizon of the vale, and already the outlines of the woods and of the farther hills were becoming indistinct in a blue evening haze.

The "Maestro" went off like a bullet, his hatchet face set in the determined way that meant business. His time came through surprisingly quickly, Arthur Day's usually quiet voice raised with excitement. It was two-fifths of a second better than his previous run.

Now Von Eberstraum! The silver Rheinwagen was pushed up to the line by the impassive German mechanics. The driver climbed into the cockpit. One mechanic fixed the detachable steering-wheel in place, while another inserted the starting-handle in the tail. At a signal from the driver he gave one sharp flick of the wrist and the engine broke into its characteristic deep-throated roar, little puffs of black smoke spurting vertically upward from sixteen short pipes as the throttle was "blipped". Von Eberstraum looked grimly determined as he drew on his gloves and adjusted his goggles. A marshal bent towards Mr Nelson in the timing-box.

"He's out for blood," he shouted above the roar.

Mr Nelson's heart sank within him, for in a moment he realised that his nightmare of the previous night was being re-enacted before his eyes. Every detail was horribly familiar; the particular quality of the light which seemed to have suddenly become dim; a little unimportant gesture which the starter made as he acknowledged the nod from the timing-box and placed the contact shoe before the wheel.

Once more a sense of inevitably impending tragedy made him feel powerless, but mastering it, he got to his feet and hammered on the glass of the window to the consternation of his colleagues.

"Stop!" he called despairingly. "Stop him!"

Too late; the words were scarcely out of his mouth when the Rheinwagen left the line with smoking tyres and rocketed away in one terrific, sustained burst of acceleration.

Mr Nelson knew then that what he was about to hear through the headphones would not be the familiar voice of Arthur Day. He was right.

People started to run and the ambulance dashed up the course. Mercifully, perhaps, Mr Nelson did not see them; he had fainted.

The tragic duel between Volanti and Von Eberstraum was almost the sole topic of discussion in motor-racing circles for months afterwards. As usual, theories as to the cause of the disaster were legion. On only one point were the theorists unanimous. The new corner was in some obscure way highly dangerous.

First Volanti had approached the corner at a fantastic speed, crammed on his brakes, and got into a terrifying and inexplicable slide as though the road had suddenly become a sheet of ice. To the horrified spectators it looked as though a crash was inevitable, and only Volanti's uncanny skill and presence of mind can have saved him. The little man's elbows worked like flails as he fought for control. Instead of the head-on impact which seemed so inevitable, the Maturati caught the bank a glancing blow as the tail swung wide, then rocketed across to the inside as though it must surely plunge over the bank to disaster, but was corrected and held on the very brink, all in a moment of time. Finally, and before the astounded spectators had time to draw breath, the car was on the road again, the howl of the blower burst forth once more like a triumphant cry, and Volanti was gone in a flurry of turf, dust and smoke to set up his incredible record.

A marshal walked up and examined the road surface, suspecting oil, but there was none visible. Many spectators were then driven away from the corner by an appalling stench which suddenly arose. Others, oddly enough, failed to notice it.

Then came Von Eberstraum. The Rheinwagen appeared to be travelling equally rapidly, but seemed quite steady under the terrific braking, and was taking the corner very fast, but apparently under perfect control, when once more the inexplicable happened. In the middle of the corner Von Eberstraum braked suddenly and appeared to alter course, with the result that the car went completely out of control, spun round, and disappeared backwards over the bank on the inside. There was a sickening crashing and splintering as the car bounded over and over through the undergrowth until it eventually came to rest, a mangled wreck, against a great upright block of stone.

The most popular theory of the accident was that the brakes seized, the arm-chair theorists talking glibly of the fluid boiling in the brake pipes as a result of the heavy braking immediately before the corner. They ignored the fact that the braking system fitted to the car had undergone many far more gruelling tests in Grand Prix races.

There were other witnesses of the disaster who had their own shadowy inkling of the possible cause, but preferred to keep it to themselves, because they doubted the evidence of their eyes, having seen what many had apparently failed to see. As Von Eberstraum came into the corner they had fancied that something darted out from the shadow of the bank below them into the path of the car. It was only a fleeting glimpse seen out of the corners of eyes intently focused on the car alone. After the car had gone the road was deserted.

Peter Bligh was amongst those who had vague but disturbing ideas about the accident, which he decided to keep to himself.

Mr Nelson was the only person who was not in the slightest doubt as to the cause, although he, too, preferred to keep his own counsel. His first action after his recovery from a severe nervous breakdown was to order a high and unclimbable fence to be erected all round the new corner.

Some of you may have wondered, like I did, why such a promising and costly improvement of Longbury Hill should be allowed to fall into disuse so soon. I have at last managed to get the real facts from Mr Nelson and Peter Bligh. So now you know, and may draw your own conclusions. Personally, I agree with Mr Nelson. I think there is something on the inside of that fence that is best left alone.

# WHERE THE STONES GROW

## Lisa Tuttle

Lisa Tuttle (1952–) began writing science fiction, fantasy and horror during her high school years in Texas, when she also edited the science fiction fanzine *Mathom*. She published her first short story, "Stranger in the House" in 1972, and came to wider public attention with the 1981 novel *Windhaven*, co-written with George R. R. Martin. On moving to England in 1980, she became a full-time writer, and published numerous novels and short stories, as well as editing anthologies and publishing *Encyclopedia of Feminism* in 1986.

A common theme of her short stories is the *unheimlich*, which is shown to its fullest in the story presented here, originally published in 1980 in the anthology *Dark Forces*, edited by Kirby McCauley. Juxtaposing British standing stones and their folklore to the United States, the story is a slow horror with a deliciously growing sense of tension and fear.

H e saw the stone move. Smoothly as a door falling shut, it swung slightly around and settled back into the place where it had stood for centuries.

*They'll kill anyone who sees them.*

Terrified, Paul backed away, ready to run, when he saw something that didn't belong in that high, empty field which smelled of the sea. Lying half-in, half-out of the triangle formed by the three tall stones called the Sisters was Paul's father, his face bloody and his body permanently stilled.

When he was twenty-six, his company offered to send Paul Staunton to England for a special training course, the offer a token of better things to come. In a panic, Paul refused, much too vehemently. His only reason—that his father had died violently in England eighteen years before—was not considered a reason at all. Before the end of the year, Paul had been transferred away from the main office in Houston to the branch in San Antonio.

He knew he should be unhappy, but, oddly enough, the move suited him. He was still being paid well for work he enjoyed, and he found the climate and pace of life in San Antonio more congenial than that of Houston. He decided to buy a house and settle down.

The house he chose was about forty years old, built of native white limestone and set in a bucolic neighbourhood on the west side of the city. It was a simple rectangle, long and low to the ground, like a railway car. The roof was flat and the gutters and window frames peeled green paint. The four rooms offered him no more space than the average mobile home, but it was enough for him.

A yard of impressive size surrounded the house with thick green grass shaded by mimosas, pecans, a magnolia, and two massive, spreading fig trees. A chain-link fence defined the boundaries of the property, although one section at the back was torn and sagging and would have to be repaired. There were neighbouring houses on either side, also set in large yards, but beyond the fence at the back of the house was a wild mass of bushes and high weeds, ten or more undeveloped acres separating his house from a state highway.

Paul Staunton moved into his house on a day in June, a few days shy of the nineteenth anniversary of his father's death. The problems and sheer physical labour involved in moving had kept him from brooding about the past until something unexpected happened. As he was unrolling a new rug to cover the ugly chequerboard linoleum in the living room, something spilled softly out: less than a handful of grey grit, the pieces too small even to be called pebbles. Just rock-shards.

Paul broke into a sweat and let go of the rug as if it were contaminated. He was breathing quickly and shallowly as he stared at the debris.

His reaction was absurd, all out of proportion. He forced himself to take hold of the rug again and finish unrolling it. Then—he could not make himself pick them up—he took the carpet sweeper and rolled it over the rug, back and forth, until all the hard grey crumbs were gone.

It was time for a break. Paul got himself a beer from the refrigerator and a folding chair from the kitchen and went out to sit in the backyard. He stationed himself beneath one of the mimosa trees and stared out at the lush green profusion. He wouldn't even mind mowing it, he thought as he drank the beer. It was his property, the first he'd ever owned. Soon the figs would be ripe. He'd never had a fig before, except inside a cookie.

When the beer was all gone, and he was calmer, he let himself think about his father.

Paul's father, Edward Staunton, had always been lured by the thought of England. It was a place of magic and history, the land his ancestors had come from. From childhood he had dreamed of going there, but it was not until he was twenty-seven, with a wife and an eight-year-old son, that a trip to England had been possible.

Paul had a few dim memories of London, of the smell of the streets, and riding on top of a bus, and drinking sweet, milky tea—but most of these earlier memories had been obliterated by the horror that followed.

It began in a seaside village in Devon. It was a picturesque little place, but famous for nothing. Paul never knew why they had gone there.

They arrived in the late afternoon and walked through cobbled streets, dappled with slanting sun-rays. The smell of the sea was strong on the wind, and the cry of gulls carried even into the centre of town. One street had looked like a mountain to Paul, a straight drop down to the grey, shining ocean, with neatly kept stone cottages staggered on both sides. At the sight of it, Paul's mother had laughed and gasped and exclaimed that she didn't dare, not in *her* shoes, but the three of them had held hands and, calling out warnings to each other like intrepid mountaineers, the Stauntons had, at last, descended.

At the bottom was a narrow pebble beach, and steep, pale cliffs rose up on either side of the town, curving around like protecting wings.

"It's magnificent," said Charlotte Staunton, looking from the cliffs to the grey-and-white movement of the water, and then back up at the town.

Paul bent down to pick up a pebble. It was smooth and dark brown, more like a piece of wood or a nut than a stone. Then another: smaller, nearly round, milky. And then a flat black one that looked like a drop of ink. He put them in his pocket and continued to search hunched over, his eyes on the ground.

He heard his father say, "I wonder if there's another way up?" And then another voice, a stranger's, responded, "Oh, aye, there is. There is the Sisters' Way."

Paul looked up in surprise and saw an elderly man with a stick and a pipe and a little black dog who stood on the beach with them as if he'd grown there, and regarded the three Americans with a mild, benevolent interest.

"The Sisters' Way?" said Paul's father.

The old man gestured with his knobby walking stick toward the cliffs to their right. "I was headed that way myself," he said. "Would you care to walk along with me? It's an easier path than the High Street."

"I think we'd like that," said Staunton. "Thank you. But who are the Sisters?"

"You'll see them soon enough," said the man as they all began to walk together. "They're at the top."

At first sight, the cliffs had looked dauntingly steep. But as they drew closer they appeared accessible. Paul thought it would be fun to climb straight up, taking advantage of footholds and ledges he could now see, but that was not necessary. The old man led them to a narrow pathway which led gently up the cliffs in a circuitous way, turning and winding, so that it was not a difficult ascent at all. The way was not quite wide enough to walk two abreast, so the Stauntons fell into a single file after the old man, with the dog bringing up the rear.

"Now," said their guide when they reached the top. "Here we are! And there stand the Sisters."

They stood in a weedy, empty meadow just outside town—roof-tops could be seen just beyond a stand of trees about a half a mile away. And the Sisters, to judge from the old man's gesture, could be nothing more than some rough grey boulders.

"Standing stones," said Edward Staunton in a tone of great interest. He walked toward the boulders and his wife and son followed.

They were massive pieces of grey granite, each one perhaps eight feet tall, rearing out of the porous soil in a roughly triangular formation. The elder Staunton walked among them, touching them, a reverent look on his face. "These must be incredibly old," he said. He looked back at their guide and raised his voice slightly. "Why are they called the 'Sisters'?"

The old man shrugged "That's what they be."

"But what's the story?" Staunton asked. "There must be some legend—a tradition—maybe a ritual the local people perform."

"We're good Christians here," the old man said, sounding indignant. "No rituals here. We leave them stones alone!" As he spoke, the little dog trotted forward, seemingly headed for the stones, but a hand gesture from the man froze it, and it sat obediently at his side.

"But surely there's a story about how they came to be here? Why is that path we came up named after them?"

"Ah, that," said the man. "That is called the Sisters' Way because on certain nights of the year the Sisters go down that path to bathe in the sea."

Paul felt his stomach jump uneasily at those words, and he stepped back a little, not wanting to be too close to the stones. He had never heard of stones that could move by themselves, and he was fairly certain such a thing was not possible, but the idea still frightened him.

"They move!" exclaimed Staunton. He sounded pleased. "Have you ever seen them do it?"

"Oh, no. Not I, or any man alive. The Sisters don't like to be spied on. They'll kill anyone who sees them."

"Mama," said Paul, urgently. "Let's go back. I'm hungry."

She patted his shoulder absently. "Soon, dear."

"I wonder if anyone has tried," said Staunton. "I wonder where such a story comes from. When exactly are they supposed to travel?"

"Certain nights," said the old man. He sounded uneasy.

"Sacred times? Like Allhallows maybe?"

The old man looked away toward the trees and the village and he said: "My wife will have my tea waiting for me. She worries if I'm late. I'll just say good day to you then." He slapped his hip, the dog sprang up, and they walked away together, moving quickly.

"He believes it," Staunton said. "It's not just a story to him. I wonder what made him so nervous? Did he think the stones would take offence at his talking about them?"

"Maybe tonight is one of those nights," his wife said thoughtfully. "Isn't Midsummer Night supposed to be magical?"

"Let's go," said Paul again. He was afraid even to look at the stones. From the corner of his eye he could catch a glimpse of them, and it seemed to him that they were leaning toward his parents threateningly, listening.

"Paul's got a good idea," his mother said cheerfully. "I could do with something to eat myself. Shall we go?"

The Stauntons found lodging for the night in a green-shuttered cottage with a Bed and Breakfast sign hanging over the gate. It was the home of Mr and Mrs Winkle, a weathered-looking couple, who raised cats and rose bushes and treated their visitors like old friends. After the light had faded from the sky, the Stauntons sat with the Winkles in their cosy parlour and talked. Paul was given a jigsaw puzzle to work, and he sat with it in a corner, listening to the adults and hoping he would not be noticed and sent to bed.

"One thing I like about this country is the way the old legends live on," Staunton said. "We met an old man this afternoon on the beach, and he led us up a path called the Sisters' Way, and showed us the stones at the top. But I couldn't get much out of him about why the stones should be called the Sisters—I got the idea that he was afraid of them."

"Many are," said Mr Winkle equably. "Better safe than sorry."

"What's the story about those stones? Do you know it?"

"When I was a girl," Mrs Winkle offered, "people said that they were three sisters who long ago had been turned to stone for sea-bathing on the Sabbath. And so wicked were they that, instead of repenting their sin, they continue to climb down the cliff to bathe whenever they get the chance."

Mr Winkle shook his head. "That's just the sort of tale you might expect from a minister's daughter," he said. "Bathing on the Sabbath indeed! That's not the story at all. I don't know all the details of it—different folks say it different ways—but there were once three girls who made the mistake of staying overnight in that field, long before there was a town here. And when morning came, the girls had turned to stone.

"But even as stones they had the power to move at certain times of the year, and so they did. They wore away a path down the cliff by going to the sea and trying to wash away the stone that covered them. But even though the beach now is littered with little bits of the stone that the sea has worn away, it will take them till doomsday to be rid of it all." Mr Winkle picked up his pipe and began to clean it.

Staunton leaned forward in his chair. "But why should spending the night in that field cause them to turn to stone?"

"Didn't I say? Oh, well, the name of that place is the place where the stones grow. And that's what it is. Those girls just picked the wrong time and the wrong place to rest, and when the stones came up from the ground the girls were covered by them."

"But that doesn't make sense," Staunton said. "There are standing stones all over England—I've read a lot about them. And I've never heard a story like that. People don't just turn to stone for no reason."

"Of course not, Mr Staunton. I didn't say it was for no reason. It was the place they were in, and the time. I don't say that sort of thing—people turning into stones—happens in this day, but I don't say it doesn't. People avoid that place where the stones grow, even though it lies so close upon the town. The cows don't graze there, and no one would build there."

"You mean there's some sort of a curse on it?"

"No, Mr Staunton. No more than an apple orchard or an oyster bed is cursed. It's just a place where stones grow."

"But stones don't grow."

"Edward," murmured his wife warningly.

But Mr Winkle did not seem to be offended by Staunton's bluntness. He smiled. "You're a city man, aren't you, Mr Staunton? You know, I heard a tale once about a little boy in London who believed the greengrocer made vegetables out of a greenish paste and baked them, just the way his mother made biscuits. He'd never seen them growing—he'd never seen *anything* growing, except flowers in window boxes, and grass in the parks—and grass and flowers aren't good to eat, so how should he know?

"But the countryman knows that everything that lives grows, following its own rhythm, whether it is a tree, a stone, a beast, or a man."

"But a stone's not alive. It's not like a plant or an animal." Staunton cast about for an effective argument. "You could prove it for yourself. Take a rock, from that field or anywhere else, and put it on your windowsill and watch it for ten years, and it wouldn't grow a bit!"

"You could try that same experiment with a potato, Mr Staunton," Mr Winkle responded. "And would you then tell me that a potato, because it didn't grow in ten years on my windowsill, never grew and never grows? There's a place and a time for everything. To everything there is a season," he said, reaching over to pat his wife's hand. "As my wife's late father was fond of reminding us."

As a child, Paul Staunton had been convinced that the stones had killed his father. He had been afraid when his mother had sent him out into the chilly, dark morning to find his father and bring him back to have breakfast, and when he had seen the stone, still moving, he had known. Had known, and been afraid that the stones would pursue him, to punish him for his knowledge, the old man's warning echoing in his mind. *They'll kill anyone who sees them.*

But as he had grown older, Paul had sought other, more rational, explanations for his father's death. An accident. A mugging. An escaped lunatic. A coven of witches, surprised at their rites. An unknown enemy who had trailed his father for years. But nothing, to Paul, carried the conviction of his first answer. That the stones themselves had killed his father, horribly and unnaturally moving, crushing his father when he stood in their way.

It had grown nearly dark as he brooded, and the mosquitoes were beginning to bite. He still had work to do inside. He stood up and folded the chair, carrying it in one hand, and walked toward the door. As he reached it, his glance fell on the window ledge beside him. On it were three light-coloured pebbles.

He stopped breathing for a moment. He remembered the pebbles he had picked up on that beach in England, and how they had come back to haunt him more than a week later, back at home in the United States, when they fell out of the pocket where he had put them so carelessly. Nasty reminders of his father's death, then, and he had stared at them, trembling violently, afraid to pick them up. Finally he had called his mother, and she had gotten rid of them for him somehow. Or perhaps she had kept them—Paul had never asked.

But that had nothing to do with these stones. He scooped them off the ledge with one hand, half-turned, and flung them away as far as he could. He thought they went over the sagging back fence, but he could not see where, amid the shadows and the weeds, they fell.

He had done a lot in two days, and Paul Staunton was pleased with himself. All his possessions were inside and in their place, the house was clean, the telephone had been installed, and he had fixed the broken latch on the bathroom window. Some things remained to be done—he needed a dining-room table, he didn't like the wallpaper in the bathroom, and the backyard would have to be mowed very soon—but all in all he thought he had a right to be proud of what he had done. There was still some light left in the day, which made it worthwhile to relax outside and enjoy the cooler evening air.

He took a chair out, thinking about the need for some lawn furniture, and put it in the same spot where he had sat before, beneath the gentle mimosa. But this time, before sitting down, he began to walk around the yard, pacing off his property and luxuriating in the feeling of being a landowner.

Something pale, glimmering in the twilight, caught his eye, and Paul stood still, frowning. It was entirely the wrong colour for anything that should be on the other side of the fence, amid that tumbled blur of greens and browns. He began to walk toward the back fence, trying to make out what it was, but was able only to catch maddeningly incomplete glimpses. Probably just trash, paper blown in from the road, he thought, but still... He didn't trust his weight to the sagging portion of the fence, but climbed another section. He paused at the top, not entirely willing to climb over, and strained his eyes for whatever it was and, seeing it at last, nearly fell off the fence.

He caught himself in time to make it a jump, rather than an undignified tumble, but at the end of it he was on the other side of the fence and his heart was pounding wildly.

Standing stones. Three rocks in a roughly triangular formation.

He wished he had not seen them. He wanted to be back in his own yard. But it was too late for that. And now he wanted to be sure of what he had seen. He pressed on through the high weeds and thick plants, burrs catching on his jeans, his socks, and his T-shirt.

There they were.

His throat was tight and his muscles unwilling, but Paul made himself approach and walk around them. Yes, there were three standing stones, but beyond the formation, and the idea of them, there was no real resemblance to the rocks in England. These stones were no more than four feet high, and less than two across. Unlike the standing stones of the Old World, these had not been shaped and set in their places—they were just masses of native white limestone jutting out of the thin soil. San Antonio lies on the Edwards Plateau, a big slab of limestone laid down as ocean sediment during the Cretaceous, covered now with seldom more than a few inches of soil. There was nothing unusual about these stones, and they had nothing to do with the legends of growing, walking stones in another country.

Paul knew that. But, as he turned away from the stones and made his way back through the underbrush to his own yard, one question nagged him, a problem he could not answer to his own satisfaction, and that was: Why didn't I see them before?

Although he had not been over the fence before, he had often enough walked around the yard—even before buying the house—and once had climbed the fence and gazed out at the land on the other side.

Why hadn't he seen the stones then? They were visible from the fence, so why hadn't he seen them more than a week earlier? He should have seen them. If they were there.

But they must have been there. They couldn't have popped up out of the ground overnight; and why should anyone transport stones to such an unlikely place? They must have been there. So why hadn't he seen them before?

*The place where the stones grow,* he thought.

Going into the house, he locked the back door behind him.

The next night was Midsummer Eve, the anniversary of his father's death, and Paul did not want to spend it alone.

He had drinks with a pretty young woman named Alice Croy after work—she had been working as a temporary secretary in his office—and then took her out to dinner, and then for more drinks, and then, after a minor altercation about efficiency, saving gas, and who was not too drunk to drive, she followed him in her own car to his house where they had a mutually satisfying if not terribly meaningful encounter.

Paul was drifting off to sleep when he realised that Alice had gotten up and was moving about the room.

He looked at the clock: it was almost two.

"What're you doing?" he asked drowsily.

"You don't have to get up." She patted his shoulder kindly, as if he were a dog or a very old man.

He sat up and saw that she was dressed except for her shoes. "What are you doing?" he repeated.

She sighed. "Look, don't take this wrong, okay? I like you. I think what we had was really great, and I hope we can get together again. But I just don't feel comfortable in a strange bed. I don't know you well enough to—it would be awkward in the morning for both of us. So I'm just going on home."

"So that's why you brought your own car."

"Go back to sleep. I didn't mean to disturb you."

"Your leaving disturbs me."

She made a face.

Paul sighed and rubbed his eyes. It would be pointless to argue with her. And, he realised, he didn't like her very much—on any other night he might have been relieved to see her go.

"All right," he said. "If you change your mind, you know where I live."

She kissed him lightly. "I'll find my way out. You go back to sleep, now."

But he was wide awake, and he didn't think he would sleep again that night. He was safe in his own bed, in his own house, surely. If his father had been content to stay inside, instead of going out alone, in the grey, predawn light, to look at three stones in a field, he might be alive now.

It's over, thought Paul. Whatever happened, happened long ago, and to my father, not me. (But he had seen the stone move.)

He sat up and turned on the light before that old childhood nightmare could appear before him: the towering rocks lumbering across the grassy field to crush his father. He wished he knew someone in San Antonio well enough to call at this hour. Someone to visit. Another presence to keep away the nightmares. Since there was no one, Paul knew that he would settle for lots of Jack Daniel's over ice, with Bach on the stereo—supreme products of civilisation to keep the ghosts away.

But he didn't expect it to work.

In the living room, sipping his drink, the uncurtained glass of the windows disturbed him. He couldn't see out, but the light in the room cast his reflection onto the glass, so that he was continually being startled by his own movements. He settled that by turning out the lights. There was a full moon, and he could see well enough by the light that it cast, and the faint glow from the stereo console. The windows were tightly shut and the air-conditioning unit was labouring steadily: the cool, laundered air and the steady hum shut out the night even more effectively than the Brandenburg Concerti.

Not for the first time, he thought of seeing a psychiatrist. In the morning he would get the name of a good one. Tough on a young boy to lose his father, he thought, killing his third drink. So much worse for the boy who finds his father's dead body in mysterious circumstances. But one had to move beyond that. There was so much more to life than the details of an early trauma.

As he rose and crossed the room for another drink (silly to have left the bottle all the way over there, he thought), a motion from the yard outside caught his eye, and he slowly turned his head to look.

It wasn't just his reflection that time. There had been something moving in the far corner of the yard, near the broken-down fence. But now that he looked for it, he could see nothing. Unless, perhaps, was that something there in the shadows near one of the fig trees? Something about four feet high, pale-coloured, and now very still?

Paul had a sudden urge, which he killed almost at once, to take a flashlight and go outside, to climb the fence and make sure those three rocks were still there. *They want me to come out,* he thought—and stifled that thought, too.

He realised he was sweating. The air conditioner didn't seem to be doing much good. He poured himself another drink and pulled his chair around to face the window. Then he sat there in the dark, sipping his whiskey and staring out into the night. He didn't bother to replace the record when the stereo clicked itself off, and he didn't get up for another drink when his glass was empty. He waited and watched for nearly an hour, and he saw nothing in the dark yard move. Still he waited, thinking, *They have their own time, and it isn't ours. They grow at their own pace, in their own place, like everything else alive.*

Something was happening, he knew. He would soon see the stones move, just as his father had. But he wouldn't make his father's mistake and get in their way. He wouldn't let himself be killed.

Then, at last—he had no idea of the time now—the white mass in the shadows rippled, and the stone moved, emerging onto the moonlit grass. Another stone was behind it, and another. Three white rocks moving across the grass.

They were flowing. The solid white rock rippled and lost its solid contours and re-formed again in another place, slightly closer to the house. Flowing—not like water, like rock.

Paul thought of molten rock and of lava flows. But molten rock did not start and stop like that, and it did not keep its original form intact, forming and re-forming like that. He tried to comprehend what he was seeing. He knew he was no longer drunk. How could a rock move? Under great heat or intense pressure, perhaps. What were rocks? Inorganic material, but made of atoms like everything else. And atoms could change, could be changed—forms could change—

But the simple fact was that rocks did not move. Not by themselves. They did not wear paths down cliffs to the sea. They did not give birth. They did not grow. They did not commit murder. They did not seek revenge.

Everyone knew this, he thought, as he watched the rocks move in his backyard. No one had ever seen a rock move.

*Because they kill anyone who sees them.*

They had killed his father, and now they had come to kill him.

Paul sprang up from his chair, overturning it, thinking of escape. Then he remembered. He *was* safe. Safe inside his own home. His hand came down on the windowsill and he stroked it. Solid walls between him and those things out there: walls built of sturdy, comforting stone.

Staring down at his hand on the white rock ledge, a half-smile of relief still on his lips, he saw it change. The stone beneath his hand rippled and crawled. It felt to his fingertips like warm putty. It was living. It flowed up to embrace his hand, to engulf it, and then solidified. He screamed and tried to pull his hand free. He felt no physical pain, but his hand was buried firmly in the solid rock, and he could not move it.

He looked around in terror and saw that the walls were now molten and throbbing. They began to flow together. A stream of living rock surged across the window-glass. Dimly, he heard the glass shatter. The walls were merging, streaming across floor and ceiling, greedily filling all the empty space. The living, liquid rock lapped about his ankles, closing about him, absorbing him, turning him to stone.

2018

# THE SUPPELL STONE

## *Elsa Wallace*

Elsa Wallace was born in Central Africa in 1939, before moving to London, where she lived until her death in 2018. Among other ventures, she was a campaigner and organiser of a number of disabled and LGBT groups, and was involved in the animal rights movement. She had several collections, novellas and a novel published by Paradise Press, including two collections of supernatural stories, *The Monkey Mirror and Other Stories* (2011) and *Ghosts and Gargoyles* (2013). She was also a longtime supporter of the M. R. James journal *Ghosts and Scholars*, in which she had two short stories published. The story included here, from issue number 34, tells of a standing stone, lone survivor of an older circle, which may have its own means of protecting itself...

**W**hether the oddments of superstition my mother told us when we were young were believed by her or were meant as a kind of amusement for us, like the Easter Bunny, Moss Babies and the Tooth Fairy, I am undecided; possibly something of both. She wouldn't wear green (but that was due to family history: Great-Aunt Emma had an emerald green dress and her fiancé had perished at sea); Christmas decorations had to be totally removed by Twelfth Night as witches could get into the least scrap of tinsel or coloured paper. The snippets of lore were varied: never bring into the house bones, peacock feathers or may blossom; never mix red and white flowers in a vase (death ensued if you did); don't look at the moon through glass; don't put shoes on a table (surely just hygienic advice); sing before morning and you'll cry before night; if you meet a piebald horse, make a cross in the dust on your shoe. The latter instruction was never observed by me; born and brought up in Central Africa I encountered no horses, because of the tsetse fly menace, and at age four on holiday in South Africa I was stunned to see a donkey pull a cart. It looked surreal.

My parents, both Londoners, had emigrated to Africa in the thirties. My father was estranged from his relatives but my mother kept in touch with her sisters, and I was twenty before I came to London and met them and a few cousins.

Great-grandfather Ford had been a farmer in the West Country, near Suppell Hill at Puttsford, and his fourteen children had scattered to the colonies leaving the eldest, Arthur, managing the land with all its troubles. Some had done well in Canada and America, two had died in the Rand goldfields, some were never heard of once they went to sea. Bess stayed to keep house for Arthur. Florence, Emily and Kate married. My mother's father who, she told us, had been taken out of school each year to do bird-scaring in the fields, so hated it that as soon as he could he escaped to London where he did surprisingly well at taking on a little shop and making enough to support wife and four children. Perhaps it was he who'd passed on the pieces of country advice such as "Never go to sleep with the moon shining on you—or you'll wake not knowing your ABC from a cow's tail".

But not in all her "reminiscences" did my mother mention the Suppell Stone. Did she know about it, or did she think it unsuitable? I remember she once glued together two pages of Grimms' Fairy Tales as she thought the illustration would give us nightmares. I knew that as a child she'd been on holiday a few times at the old place and had slept in a tent when there were too many for the cottage. She'd said she didn't know how the cottage had held her father and all his siblings. Two of the older boys went to sea very young. I mightn't have known of the Stone if I hadn't happened to mention to Cousin Edie that I planned to see Stonehenge and Avebury. After I'd met the London relatives and surfeited on the city, I had a fancy to visit Puttsford, our fountainhead as it seemed. My aunts were doubtful: "There's little to see there now. The Rannans took most of the farm when Arthur's boy couldn't keep it going. Edie's still got the cottage, of course, and a bit of garden. We don't know what you'll make of her. She's more a Putt than a Ford. It's quite primitive still, water from the well, privy at the end of the garden. We don't know why she stays, at her age. She'll have to move one of these days. We had to bully her to get the phone".

Aunt Patty said, "Lizzie won't mind primitive, June! She's from Africa".

I hesitated to explain I'd had modern plumbing all my life; the mine estates looked after their white employees at least, and I didn't tell them what a surprise London had been to me—rationing and bomb sites, for a start.

Cousin Edie, unlike my mother and her sisters, was plump, prettily rounded. In a loose, comfortable dove-grey dress and with her thick white hair in a knot at the nape of her neck, she suited her surroundings. The cottage was basic, functional: strong walls, tiny windows, flagged floor. I thought modernising would spoil it. Ceilings were low and I had to stoop to enter but I believe people were shorter then. The little garden was charming with its well and discreetly screened "small room" in a corner.

We had a sandwich lunch in the kitchen with the open door showing a hedge of fuchsias. At first our talk was awkward: a few questions about Africa, what was it like and now I'd seen London wouldn't I choose to stay? I said the Festival of Britain was memorable, the ballet especially, but I'd found the traffic in Oxford Street unpleasant.

Edie was more travelled than I had been at that time: she'd been to San Francisco and Hong Kong with her son and his wife, but hadn't thought much of either.

Conversation faded intermittently. A diversion was a bold hen who looked in on us to peck Edie's shoe. We resorted to the good old standby, the photograph album. Many pictures were of children in Victorian or Edwardian dress and I was soon lost in the welter of names. Notable was Emma posed at a roll-top desk, perhaps wearing the fateful green, and Matty half-blind from birth who did much of the milking and who'd said the cows either like you or they don't, and Daisy would only let her milk down for Matty. There was my mother looking jaunty and boyish in shorts, hammering in tent pegs, her father whittling at a piece of applewood; Bess who was so well-padded she could ride a horse without a saddle. One (to my mind, sad) group picture of ten of the fourteen looking solemn, from teenagers to toddlers. Was it one of the few times all were together?

We were getting on happily when there was a knock at the front door. Edie sighed, "That'll be old Perce. I'm sorry for that. He does like the sound of his own voice. At least I've trained him not to come round the side—not since he caught me in my petti. He thinks I'll marry him but I won't. I'm not daft."

She let him knock a few times. To my eyes he was too old to think of marriage, though spry enough, wiry and tanned. Later he boasted to me that he walked everywhere and one could believe it, his polished walking-stick as much part of him as his stout boots.

He came in chuckling and, with a nod to me, said, "I just been up at Giltons and the leopard's been seen again".

"What nonsense. It was just a big cat. Would you like some tea?"

"That was no moggie, Charlie said. It was over the gate so he could measure it by that. Four foot long if it was an inch. Small head. Long tail."

"Perce, sit down. This is Lizzie, Cousin Jean's girl, you know, I told you, from Africa, so you can forget telling her about leopards."

I'd never seen a leopard in the wild.

"Africa," said Perce, seating himself. "I used to know a chap went to Cape Town, for the railways."

I said I was only a Rhodesian.

Perce sought to sing for his tea and scone with local news which meant nothing to me except for one item: the Tom Putt apple tree on the part of the farm now owned by Bicknells was to be cut down.

Edie was distressed and told me, "That tree was planted the day your great uncle Joe sailed for America; it's more than a hundred years."

"Yes, well, it's all change." He gave a chuckle. "Of course, we all know Joe left a baby in Rosie Bicknell before he went, so there's still Fords there."

Edie frowned at him and changed the subject. "Lizzie's going to Stonehenge. A visitor always sees more. All the years of my life and I've never been. Never will now. Strange, isn't it, to have seen the Golden Gate. We used to have a circle up Suppell Hill but that's gone."

"There's still the Suppell Stone," said Perce replenishing his teacup familiarly. "You could see that. I'll take you up there myself."

"You will not." Edie was sharp, and to me she said, "It's on Mr Rannan's grounds and he's very private. He won't let in anyone. Jenny at the library told me last year a historian came wanting to see it, from Ilminster, and Mr Rannan refused him. And before that, the photographer doing a book. Sent him off with a flea in his ear. He won't have anyone near the place. What about the hiker last summer, put up his tent on the hillside and Willis drove him off. He was quite rough about it."

"*I* could get you in," said Perce confidently. "Mr Rannan's not there, away on his travels again. There's just the stepson, Sebastian."

"I hope *you* don't call him that." Edie was severe.

"And why not? He's just a youngster to me. As for Willis, I'd smack his legs for him and he knows it." He turned to me. "How long're you here? I can take you to the old stone, no trouble at all."

Edie uttered a sound of disbelief.

"There's just the big fellow left, the Suppell Stone. In the old days there was a ring, like Edie said, but they were broken up and taken off. They wanted the squire to get rid of the big one but he wouldn't. They burned the old house but his son just put up a new one. You can still see the hollows where the ring stones were, the smaller ones."

"How can she see them?" Edie was scornful. "It's all planted over now, the rhododendrons gone mad, and besides it's out of bounds for the likes of us. For the likes of anyone actually. He opens the gardens one day a year but that's the other side and nothing to see but green. They say he's got almost every tree and shrub there is."

Perce went on, "You should see it, if you like history. It's our one landmark aside from the church. Old Rannan's away, it'll be a doddle. There's a story attached, Jean's girl, better than Stonehenge to my mind. They can keep their Druids. This is better because true.

"Long while back the tinkers used to come and have their horses on that hill when it was all grass. Their kids played up there and then one evening the littlest girl disappeared and the rest of them scared out of their wits which is saying something. Those kids were tough. They wouldn't talk at first but at last they got it out of them. Her two brothers saw it all. They said the big stone folded her up. She'd got too near. It wrapped her up in itself. It swallowed her up like she was supper."

Edie sighed. "And when is this supposed to have happened? Eh? What king was on the throne, tell me that. As I said, it's a story that grows. Nowadays, when a child is missing we know what to think, sadly, and it would have been the same then, whenever that was."

Perce pressed on. "They never came back after that. They wanted the squire to smash the stone, but he set a guard on it, a sort of animal maybe, with a savage hunger, and stones put over it to hold it—that was the time of the old religion. But we still knew not to be there after dark."

Edie laughed and began to stack dishes in the sink. I was anxious to be away. She was looking tired and I'd seen a secondhand shop in the village that might be worth investigating, just for fun.

"Of course we were told that—because our mums wanted us in for our supper."

"Yes," Perce confirmed, "and we called it the Supper Stone. We used to say:

> "Supper Stone, Supper Stone,
> Eat you up, flesh and bone."

"*Who* used to say?" Edie demanded. "Not I!"

"You must remember. Or maybe it was just us boys. We used to dare each other to go up there. Double-dare to touch it. And then we'd run away. Yes, I wouldn't mind seeing the old Supper Stone again."

"You can see it alone then," Edie said shortly.

I'd booked a room overnight at the Fox to save her the trouble of putting me up, and used my wish for a bath as my excuse to be on my way, adding I was sure to be back to see her once more.

"I'll walk down with you," said Perce (Edie rolled her eyes), and on our stroll back I think he hardly drew breath. I heard about Mr Rannan and his globe-trotting, his marriage to a lovely young widow, Sebastian's mother. She had vanished one day. He, Perce, had his opinion about that. So had I: young woman, older man, dull country life after Madrid, but Perce enjoyed alluding to the power of the Stone. I forbore to point to the inconsistency of people clamouring for the Stone's destruction if it was supposed to hold in check the voracious beast beneath it.

After I'd done Stonehenge and been to Callanish and Hadrian's Wall and before getting the *Llangibby Castle* home, I did visit Edie again, giving her a nice silver thistle brooch; but Perce was there so we didn't have the continuation of talk I'd hoped for, with his frequent interruptions. And I was peeved when, as before, he walked with me back into the village.

I was thinking how to shake him off as we came into the High Street—I needed to book a taxi for the station—when, waving his stick, he called loudly to a man emerging from the post office: "Sebastian! Well met, just the man I want to see. I've got Lizzie with me, Edie Putt's cousin. From Rhodesia!"

The man turned slowly. Tall and slender, perhaps in his thirties, he didn't respond to Perce's greeting except to raise an eyebrow. His narrow pale face looked blanched in contrast with his neat dark hair.

Perce was undeterred. "She's been to Stonehenge and Avebury, she's that interested in the old stones so she'll like to see the old Supper—Suppell Stone. Edie and me's told her all about it."

The man regarded him without a flicker of expression.

I said something like, "No, please, I don't really, I must be going".

He didn't look at me; instead there was a faintly aloof smile and he said very quietly, "By all means. But Willis locks the gate at five".

"It's hardly four now," said irrepressible Perce. "Plenty of time."

"If you say so," in a murmur almost under his breath. He gave a nod and as he turned away added, "Of course you know not to tamper with anything".

I'd have been indignant but perhaps Perce didn't hear him, already striding off. It was no distance up the slope from the village, with a thick hedge on the left side. The black and gilt carriage gates were locked but the small side gate grudgingly let itself be pushed open.

"Now," said my escort, surveying the scene. "I judge we go this way."

"Don't you *know*? I don't feel happy wandering about on someone else's property."

"It wasn't always theirs. In the old days we could come and go."

The aspect wasn't inviting: the drive was two ruts divided by a grassy ribbon leading off to the right, round a sturdy growth of trees which must have been concealing the house. A great stretch of grass was well mown and to the left where the ground rose significantly, huge rhododendrons seemed to prevent any ingress. But Perce's instinct or memory was true and, beckoning, he led me toward this thickly overgrown wilderness to find a path, narrow and gravelled, leading straight upwards through it.

It isn't hindsight to note I was at once uneasy proceeding between the towering growths of dark green. Our footsteps on the gravel sounded unnaturally loud. I suppose the thickset bushes acted as a baffle to any other sounds. Perce was unaffected, humming, but was silent when we reached the summit and patch of open sward, in the far corner of which was the Stone backed by the strong wall of stout bushes. In fact we were walled in by this rampant vegetation but for the entrance from the gravel path.

"It's a monster, isn't it?" said Perce. "You can see why they wanted rid of it."

At first I thought "No I can't", but on consideration I recognised that it made us look puny and inferior, and wasn't that partly the reason humans murdered elephants, not only for their riches but because they overshadowed us and diminished us? The height and weight of this stone might inspire fear and anger on that account alone. I felt intimidated by its sense of its own presence (as it seemed to me), and because the area of close-cropped turf before it wasn't extensive and I couldn't stand back as far from it as I'd have wished. In fact, involuntarily I had taken a step away.

I was therefore surprised at Perce's action in slapping his hand firmly on it, as though it were a horse.

"Pity you haven't got your camera. The light's not bad."

I knew at once I wouldn't have photographed it. It wasn't at all what I'd expected: not a rough chunk, pitted, jagged, a greyish or off-white slab. No, here was something quite other: pear-shaped, rounded smooth with a matt surface, perhaps eight feet high and three feet across at the base, dark grey, almost black in places with a vein of faint reddish hue down the right side. The smoothness of it made me think of a picture I'd seen of a stone lion somewhere in Asia (I think) which had been caressed over the centuries by thousands of hands for good luck so that its face and paws were blunted. The Suppell Stone had a look of that and yet—yet who would touch it, for it was so massy and overpowering.

Perce would. He supported himself against it and with his stick rummaged in the turf at its foot.

"Wonder how deep it goes. Must be some way. Billy Ryles said he buried a marble here. I says to him I'll believe that when I see the marble."

My alarm increased as he continued to probe away with the ferrule, but I couldn't define why. I hadn't felt this at Stonehenge which I'd naturally found most impressive, nor at Hadrian's Wall, nor at Callanish; there my thoughts had been chiefly of those who'd once lived and worked there. They didn't awe me as this did.

In Rhodesia I'd been to Great Zimbabwe, of course, and had marvelled at the fine stonework; and at Inyanga I'd seen majestic rock formations weathered into shapes that had earned them names, like Crusader, Punch and Fox Rocks, all part of the landscape and unmenacing.

Here in this enclosed space I had intimations of hostility. It was so quiet but for Perce's scrapings. I couldn't understand his insouciance, this asserting of himself, his indifference, apparently, to the strength of the thing. Was he showing off?

"I think there's some marks here," he said, stooping and pushing earth away with his foot. "Look. See what I mean?"

I didn't move, and said I'd seen enough and we should go. And then I heard the noise, like the sea, like waves washing pebbles to and fro. It was a sound I recalled from a visit to Brighton. The wash on African beaches with their thick sand is different.

"Come on, I'm going," I said, and at that moment heard the crunch of gravel and, stepping back to the path, saw Sebastian advancing slowly up the slope with, behind him, a sturdy man in shirtsleeves who looked like a gardener.

Sebastian halted and looked at me impassively.

I said hastily, "We're just leaving. Thank you so much for letting us see it", and retreated a little, calling to Perce as I did so.

He wasn't there. But for his walking stick the place was empty. I was utterly bewildered and called again and again. The tall bushes were so close-set, as if they'd stitched themselves together, that he couldn't have slipped away into them nor got behind the stone. There would have been sounds of anyone forcing his way into that entanglement. There was no sign of disturbance in the green barrier.

I was most discomfited and said something like "I'm so sorry, I can't make it out, I don't know where he can be, he was right here", feeling foolish and unwelcome.

The man, Willis as it transpired, came up and past me, and then returning to Sebastian said something in a low tone.

Sebastian gave a small cold smile and said, "I'm afraid Willis wants to lock up. If you wouldn't mind..." and made a slight gesture to usher me down. Checking my watch I saw it was a few minutes to five. This was impossible—we couldn't have been here all that time. I looked round behind me once more and then went down slowly and unwillingly, glancing back in hopes Perce would appear.

But he never did. Later I blamed myself for leaving without him. I should have insisted on remaining. But I was embarrassed, and after all they both knew Perce and perhaps he was playing some sort of joke on them; perhaps he had managed, somehow, to squeeze into that seemingly impenetrable hedge. Edie was no letter writer and I was home in Lusaka for some time before learning via the aunts that hope to see Edie's old friend again had been abandoned. The consequence of several searches of the area was only to infuriate Mr Rannan at the breach of his privacy.

I've voiced my suspicions to no one. One scene plays over in my mind. When I was escorted (evicted?) by the two men, wordlessly (and civilly, I suppose I must admit) from the estate and out into the roadway, I had hesitated, waiting until the last minute to leave.

Willis locked the smaller gate with a large black key which he placed in a canvas bag at his waist.

Slightly to his rear and as if he had forgotten my presence, Sebastian leaned a little toward him and said softly, "Well, we know the Giltons' leopard cannot have taken him, don't we?"

Through the bars I could see Willis's brief sardonic smile.

For more Tales of the Weird titles
visit the British Library Shop (shop.bl.uk)

We welcome any suggestions, corrections or feedback you may have, and will
aim to respond to all items addressed to the following:

The Editor (Tales of the Weird), British Library Publishing,
The British Library, 96 Euston Road, London NWI 2DB

We also welcome enquiries through our Twitter account, @BL_Publishing.